MERRY ME

A HOLIDAY ROMANCE NOVEL

AMANDA SIEGRIST

Copyright © 2016 Amanda Siegrist
All Rights Reserved.

This material may not be re-produced, re-formatted, or copied in any format for sale or personal use unless given permission by the publisher.

All characters in this book are a product of the author's imagination. Places, events, and locations mentioned either are created to help inspire the story or are real and used in a fictitious manner.

Note: The towns mentioned in this story are fictitious, except for St. Cloud. That is a real city in Minnesota full of culture, beauty, and kindness. You should visit it someday.

Cover Designer: Amanda Siegrist
Photos provided by: Syda Productions/Shutterstock.com

ISBN-13: 978-1546911067
ISBN-10: 1546911065

ALSO BY AMANDA SIEGRIST

A happy ending is all I need.

Holiday Romance Novel
Mistletoe Magic
Christmas Wish
Snowed in Love
Snowflakes and Shots

McCord Family Novel
Protecting You
Trust in Love
Deserving You
Always Kind of Love

Perfect For You Novel
The Wrong Brother

Lucky Town Novel
Escaping Memories
Dangerous Memories
Stolen Memories

Consequences Novel
Dark Consequences

One Taste Novel

One Taste of You

One Taste of Love

One Taste of Crazy

One Taste of Sin

One Taste of Redemption

Standalone Novel

The Danger with Love

Mona & Mason

The Paranormal Chronicles

Conquering Fear Novel

Co-written with Jane Blythe

Drowning in You

Out of the Darkness

MERRY CHRISTMAS.

MAY YOUR DAYS AND NIGHTS BE FILLED WITH HOLIDAY CHEER!

1

"Merry Christmas, Chief," Bernie from the hardware store said as Chief Elliot Duncan strolled by.

"Hey, Bernie. How's the family?" Elliot slowed his pace even as his feet itched to reach his car and drive as far away from Mulberry as he could.

"Just fine. James is dying to have that new racecar thingamajig, so I have to head to the store after work. Hope they're not sold out." Bernie laughed, wiping a hand over his forehead as if he hoped to dodge a bullet.

Elliot laughed as well. "Good luck, Bernie. Have a nice day."

"You, too, Chief."

Elliot kept walking, as his truck loomed closer. Just a few more steps to freedom. How many times would people wish him a merry Christmas today? It wasn't that merry. Oh, he played it off well enough that everything was merry, hunky-dory, and all that fine jazz. But he couldn't stand Christmas since the day his mother passed away three years ago. And for some reason, because she didn't pass away near the holidays, he always thought of his mom this time of year.

Probably because she always managed to make it bright and merry from day one. Baking delicious treats, stopping by at the police station almost every day, dropping off cookies, cakes, pies, and every other treat she had felt that he and the other officers would enjoy. Heck, many of the townsfolk had been aware of the delicious treats she made and knew they were welcome to the wonderful baked goods as well. He hadn't even been chief then, just another officer in the building. That hadn't mattered to her; she still stopped by making nice with everyone.

And his parents' house, the wonderful smell of cinnamon that hit his nose every time he walked through the front door, or the Christmas music that would be lightly playing in the background. Sure, his mom probably had the TV on as well. It didn't matter. She wanted to hear the joyous music all the time.

She loved Christmas. That made him love Christmas. Now she was gone. What was the point? It'd be better if the holiday never existed.

No more visits with treats to the station. No more cinnamon wafting to his nose, especially since his dad sold the house and moved in with him. No more Christmas music just for the hell of it.

His dad tried to make this time of the year special, but Elliot would slap the off button to the radio with a flick of his wrist or barely glance at the burnt cookies his dad always attempted to bake. He could hide his feelings about the holiday to everyone—except his dad.

Sighing heavily as he pulled the truck door open, the point of the holiday was to make it merry for his dad. He missed her just as much as Elliot did. She had been an amazing woman.

"Merry Christmas, Elliot."

Looking over the truck door, Marybeth Jenkins stood on the sidewalk in her dashing red-velvet coat and black high heels. His eyes drifted over her form, her coat grabbing his attention as nothing else peeked out from underneath. It left a man to his imagination. Marybeth had a nice body. She displayed it often enough with seductive, form-fitting clothes. Not that it ever enticed him. He didn't want a woman this time of year, especially Marybeth. Too loud in her wardrobe, too forward in her advances. That sort of personality made him cringe.

"Hi, Marybeth."

"Care to join me for lunch?"

"Thanks for the offer, but I'm going home for lunch. I told my dad I'd be there."

Her face dipped a little.

Out of nowhere, he offered a polite smile. Why did she keep trying? He always brushed her off. She should've gotten the hint by now that he wasn't interested.

"Rain check, then?"

"With the holidays here, it might get difficult."

"I'm a patient woman, Elliot. Have a wonderful day," she said as she sent him a sweet smile and continued walking down the sidewalk.

Elliot rushed into his seat, slamming the door before another person could stop him. Driving through town, a permanent smile and friendly wave signified the holiday spirit, even as his heart spiraled into misery. He might not appreciate Christmas anymore, but it'd take a true detective to see the real pain inside.

Ten minutes later, he pulled into his driveway. A loud

grumble from his stomach erupted as he opened his door. What could be on the menu today? Hopefully his dad didn't forget to cook. Occasionally it happened, and he'd crack jokes that his dad's age was catching up to him.

Too bad it wasn't his turn today. The burger joint he passed had made him salivate. Next week he'd enjoy the burgers when his turn came around. Thank goodness, he always made plans with his dad to have lunch. His excuses to politely shut down Marybeth were running out. She seemed eager today for his attention. He hit a good day when his dad didn't actually make other plans. Recently retired, that happened a lot.

The slam of his door didn't drown out another gurgle. He froze to regain his composure. Bringing his dad into his despair wouldn't make the day any better. Probably only bring up old arguments.

About two years after his mom died, his dad had moved in with him after he suffered a small heart attack that left Elliot nervous. He lost his mom to cancer and he hadn't been prepared to lose his dad as well. He had suggested to his dad about moving in. It took a lot of talking and finagling to get his dad to agree. The one huge argument that always surfaced from his dad was, "How are you going to meet a nice woman with an old crotchety man living with you?" He always responded back with, "You're not that old or crotchety."

At one point in time, sure, it would've been nice to find a woman and start a family. Now, the chance was too risky. The pain that always squeezed his heart every time he thought of his mother nearly made him keel over to the ground with no chance of regaining his stance. The perfect solution was to avoid that kind of pain. Keep his heart locked up to any woman.

Another protest escaped from his stomach. He took two more steps to the porch and slowed his pace again. On the small table between the rocking chair and the front door sat a present. His feet dragged as he approached the bright package. Like most things associated with Christmas, receiving presents shoved too many painful memories front and center. With any luck, it was his dad's.

The paper looked fairly old as he turned it around in his hand. A light tannish-brown background with little multi-colored presents littered in a haphazard pattern and a bright red ribbon with glittery snowflakes tied neatly around the box. His hand jerked as he zoned in on the ribbon. Tied so perfectly. So delicately. Damn, his mom would've wrapped it like that.

A small portion of white stuck out from underneath the ribbon. Carefully, he pulled out a tiny blank envelope. He turned toward the door to head inside and ask his dad who left the gift here, knowing in all reality, his dad probably set it here and just forgot. That memory of his concerned him sometimes.

The oddity of the paper, the uniqueness of the bow overtook his control as he pulled out a white card with a lovely green wreath circling the border.

MAY YOUR HOLIDAYS BE EVER BRIGHT. MAY YOUR WISHES BE EVER RIGHT. MAY THE SPIRIT OF CHRISTMAS FILL YOU WITH LOVE AND COMFORT UNTIL THE END OF NIGHT.

His brows dipped as he read the card. The words reached inside his heart, hammering once at the lock firmly in place.

No name attached. Who was the gift meant for?

A puzzle.

Maybe the answer was hidden inside. He carefully removed the bow and tore open the wrapping paper. The cover to the box was a glittering silver color, sparkling like a diamond, with a shiny silver strip of ribbon from one end to the other. The box itself was a light gray with white snowflakes and dark gray stars sprinkled around it. Why wrap such a pretty looking box? He lifted the lid to the box. The puzzle instantly morphed into a further complex mystery.

Inside, snuggled in a nice ball, was a pair of Christmas socks. The socks, patterned in red, green, and white with a fluffy white band on top, reminded him of Santa's hat. Who in the world would give him a pair of socks, Christmas ones at that? He started to put the cover back on the box when a flash of green hit his eyes. Pushing the socks aside, a nicely folded twenty-dollar bill appeared. Now, he could appreciate that gift. He had no use for the socks.

Regardless, he shoved the lid back on the box and opened the front door. His dad would know the mystery of the box. End of complication. Unless it was a secret Santa sort of thing. Did he miss a memo at work about it? Daphne, the queen of the front desk, was always trying to instill the holiday spirit every time he turned around. Pretending around her had become difficult.

Please, don't be that ridiculous tradition. He had a horrible time picking out gifts, even before his mother died.

"Hey, Dad. Where are you?" Elliot yelled, shoving the door closed behind him as he set the box down.

"In the kitchen. Is it snowing yet?"

Elliot hung up his jacket in the closet, grabbed the gift, and walked quickly to the kitchen. "No. I didn't think we had snow in the forecast."

"Yeah, the weatherman said we're supposed to be getting three to four inches come nightfall."

Elliot chuckled. "Doesn't even look like it wants to. You

know how those weather people are."

Gregory looked at Elliot as he pulled the mayo out of the fridge. "Whatchya got there? Someone give you a present?"

Elliot tossed the box onto the counter. "It was on the porch outside. Did someone stop by? There's no name on the card."

Gregory stared at the box with glazed eyes, then abruptly turned around to grab more ingredients out of the fridge. "No one stopped by that I know of. Weird."

"Yeah, it's weird. I'll wrap it back up. I just wanted to see if it said inside who it was from." Elliot sighed as the bright red ribbon grabbed his attention, its glittering snowflakes sparkling like elegant white lights on a tree.

"Why would you wrap it back up?"

A better question would be—why had he opened it up to begin with?

"Not sure when I would ever wear these socks, Dad. They look like they're for a woman. Look how long they are," Elliot said, pulling them out of the box. They hung in his hand, almost the entire length of his forearm.

"They look perfect for you. You need a bit more Christmas spirit in you, Elliot. Your mother wouldn't like how much of a Grinch you've turned into. Maybe that present was just waiting for you to unwrap."

"Dad, did you give me this ridiculous gift?"

Gregory shook his head. "Maybe it came from one of the churches in the area."

"What are you talking about?"

"You know, donating a gift to a family in need."

"I'm not someone in need," Elliot said, shoving the socks back into the box. His mystery just turned into a case like the ones that landed on his desk at work. He never walked away from those and he wasn't about to start now. There were definitely people who could use this gift, especially the twenty dollars. Not him. He had plenty of money.

"I don't know about that, son. You are in need of a lot of things," his dad said softly, grabbing the bread from the cupboard.

"Like what?"

"If you have to ask, then you're worse off than I thought. Enjoy the holidays for once. If you're so pressed to refuse such a thoughtful gift, then give it back," his dad replied as he slammed the bread on the counter.

Elliot flinched. "How? It doesn't say who it's from."

"You're the chief of police, figure it out."

He ran a hand through his hair as his dad yanked two pieces of bread out of the bag. "I didn't mean to upset you, Dad."

"What makes you think I'm upset?" his dad replied, slamming the cupboard door shut.

Elliot sighed. Why couldn't he hide his despair for the holiday better? Now the rest of lunch would be stilted as he attempted to make his dad feel better. He *would* make his father feel better before he left, even if he had to throw on Christmas music. Maybe his mom's favorite song would cheer his dad up.

The grumbling of his stomach was lost in the sound of joyous holiday music as it filled the room. A smile slowly crept up his dad's face as Elliot turned the volume up another notch.

He took a seat at the table, his back to the gift. That didn't force it out of his mind. How hard could it be to find the owner? The peculiar look in his dad's eyes at the mention of the church gave him a starting point.

❄

Lynn blew a breath up towards her bangs, resisting the urge to scream from the top of her lungs. The morning had been horrible trying to find the perfect gift, and the afternoon wasn't looking any better.

Walking toward the back supply room, she leaned against the wall as every sound from the diner melted away.

The morning had proved to be one of the most challenging she had in a while. Tis' the season to donate. Something she did every year, no matter how tight money became. Just one nice little gift to donate to the church and feel like she contributed like every other faithful churchgoer. She loved Christmas and the holiday spirit, the thought of giving a gift to a person and watching as their eyes lit up with excitement.

But, like every month, money was scarce.

Nothing dazzling had struck her eye as she roamed around her house, visiting each room like a drill sergeant inspecting the bunkhouse. No money to buy a present. And nothing worthwhile in her house. Failure had never been in her vocabulary. Something extraordinary would pop up in her house somewhere. Any nice, well-maintained thing would do.

But there was the crux of the problem. Well-maintained.

Old, worn, and from the thrift store. The very definition of her belongings. No one said it would be easy being a single mom to a seven-year-old. When had life ever been easy for her? No money for those nice pair of shoes, or the new video game that just released, or the new movie that everyone had to see. Laura, her wonderful daughter, just understood. Money was tight, and when Lynn could afford to spoil her, she would.

It wasn't often. But when she did, oh boy, what a treat. Regardless of having no money, barely able to pay the monthly rent, or sometimes scrounging for spare change just to buy food, her daughter's happiness was top priority. Her daughter deserved it. She always did her homework right away, kept her bedroom clean, rarely talked back with attitude. Such a good little girl. Too mature, really, for her age. She deserved the world.

While she may not own the fanciest or the most fashionable clothes, she had decent clothes that fit. She would stick a needle in her eye before she allowed her daughter to walk out of the house with floodwater pants or shirts that didn't reach her wrists or any clothes that were a little too tight. They were poor, but her daughter would never look poor. She drew the line at that.

Hand her a needle and thread and she'd create a masterpiece worthy in the designer world. Something she did every so often with Laura's clothes. Laura always displayed a smile and enthusiasm, giving Lynn pause at whether she was masquerading her true feelings. In the end, it didn't matter. She had no money for the really nice stuff anyway.

She had ended the torturous search in her bedroom, hoping for anything lovely to pop out and say, "Wrap me!" Except, the only thing to pierce her vision had been the twenty-dollar bill lying on her dresser. Who used money as a gift? So impersonal. Something she wasn't. Thought and care went into each gift she gave every year. And she had to buy Laura's presents.

Banging her head on the wall as the cooking sounds from the kitchen still couldn't pull her away from her turmoil, the pain radiated down her spine as it sunk in. Spineless. Taking the easy way out this year. And that twenty was now lost to another family instead of her precious daughter.

Considering there were only two more weeks until

Christmas, she only had two presents so far. She always made it a point to give Laura five. It didn't matter how she managed to do it, short of stealing, she'd never do that. But always five gifts. Faltering this year wasn't acceptable. Some extra brainstorming was in order to achieve her goal.

She had already bought a beautiful monkey watch from the zoo when they made their yearly trip to the Twin Cities. Laura's face had lit up when she saw the watch in the gift shop, and Lynn had slyly purchased it before they left. A whopping twenty-five dollars later, setting her back, of course. Just meant more overtime at the diner. Nothing new there either. But imagining Laura's excitement when the paper tore from the present and the watch was revealed, that's what mattered. Her daughter's happiness.

The second gift waiting patiently to be opened was a beautiful monkey quilt she started making last Christmas. Every time she walked into the thrift store, her eyes zeroed in on anything monkey-like. Laura just loved monkeys. Lynn knew without a doubt that she would love the quilt.

The other three gift ideas still hung in the air like mistletoe waiting for a beautiful couple to kiss underneath. What in the world would she get Laura with money she didn't have? Now that the twenty was gone, her conscience clear that she donated, her predicament just transferred into a new puzzle. Why couldn't something spectacular have popped out at her while she searched the house?

Not a stranger to extra hours and hard work at the diner, there was really only one solution. Even more extra hours and hard work than ever before. Not that it was helping her particularly at the moment. A busy morning and hardly anything to show for it. Rude outsiders that strolled through the town, demanding this and that as she broke her back to appease their every little desire. And did she receive a decent tip as gratitude? More like a slap in the face. Perhaps that was her sign she should've put more thought into the gift for the church. Karma always came around.

Two more weeks before Christmas. Positive thinking. Anything could be accomplished with an optimistic outlook. Life had taught her that.

A deep breath escaped. Picturing her daughter's face always brightened her mood. Like her excitement this morning.

"What are you doing, Mom? You've been tearing the house apart all morning. Have you found what you're looking for? Can't imagine it's hidden in your sock drawer," Laura had said, raising an eyebrow to the drawer hanging open behind Lynn.

"Just looking for, you know, stuff. Are you ready for school?"

"Yes, Mom." Laura had shuffled her feet for a millisecond before blurting, "A few of the other girls are doing secret Santa gifts this year and asked if I wanted to join in. Sounds like fun. Max spending amount is ten dollars. Can I do it, Mom?"

Laura had rushed into the room a few steps when Lynn's mouth had started to open. "I have money in my piggy bank. I already counted. I have ten dollars of my own money. I really wanna do it. Please, Mom. Please, please, please."

If there was one thing Lynn had never liked, it was Laura spending her money on other people. Now she understood it was Christmas, but like Lynn, Laura saved her money wisely to buy *herself* something special every once in a while. She'd rather give Laura ten dollars to join in on the secret Santa fun instead of using her own money.

Problem. Of course, there's always a problem. Lynn didn't have ten dollars to give her. But denying the happiness that spread across Laura's face had her saying only one thing.

"If you want to use your own money, then that's fine. We can go shopping this weekend."

Laura had grabbed her into a huge hug, squeezing tightly. "Thank you, thank you, thank you. I love you, Mom. I need to grab my bag and I'm ready to go. Hurry up, Mom. We'll be late if *you* don't hurry up."

"Shoo. I'll be right out there." Lynn had motioned for her daughter to leave, turning back toward her dresser.

That's the exact moment the twenty had disappeared into the box with a lousy pair of Christmas socks. The stress of everything had bogged her down. Wrapping the present, releasing heavy sighs in between ripping off pieces of tape, her Christmas obligation had been completed. To lighten the pain around her heart for taking the easy way out, she had written words to uplift the recipient. Her words would have to be enough to instill the Christmas spirit.

Utterly crazy. The whole ordeal.

As she had tied the ribbon, the crimson red with white shimmering snowflakes twinkling in front of her eyes, the heavy weight of guilt had pulled her down like an anchor falling to the ocean floor. That cemented the decision even further. She had donated every single year. As she would this year. She wasn't a family in need. Never once had she considered herself to be a family in need. She did just fine raising her daughter by herself and didn't need anyone's help. And curse the person who said otherwise.

When she had dropped the gift off to Father Preston, she had seen the strange look in his eyes that he wanted to deny her gift. That he had considered her to be a family in need. Of course, when he tried to persuade her to keep it, nothing but a smile graced his features.

Friendly or not, his words had fallen false to her ears. Speaking ill towards a priest, especially Father Preston, who treated her as if she were family, would turn her into her mother. Definitely not a woman she aspired to be.

Slipping out a half-truth that plenty of love and thoughtfulness went into picking out the gift, Lynn had made it impossible for him to refuse. And with one last glance at Father Preston as he had lifted the gift in goodbye, the bright red ribbon had flashed again.

Hurriedly, she had left the church before she snatched the present back. The urge had followed her each step she took to the junker of a car she proudly owned.

After arriving at the diner, about a mile away, the thought that she should voluntarily sign in to a mental ward sounded ideal. One problem after another as the shift progressed had brought the despair lower and lower.

A calming breath released as her spine steeled. No mental ward. No wishing upon a star. No lucky penny in her pocket. Only hard work and determination to make some wonderful, astronomical tips the next few days would save her Christmas.

Yeah, right. Like that was ever going to happen. The way this hectic day was going, she'd be lucky if she left in one piece.

"Hey, Lynn, I need you back out here," her co-worker Jeremy yelled down the hallway.

Lynn pushed herself off the wall, pasted her friendly diner-smile on, and walked back out to hopefully make a killing and give Laura the best Christmas ever.

The day couldn't possibly get any worse.

2

Blowing out a strained breath, Elliot took a left toward the church. He never had this much trouble solving a case before. Not that he ever had real difficult cases to handle. Living in Mulberry, population 521, didn't gain that many troubling cases. They never had any murders, a few natural deaths that still hurt to deal with, but the shock would tear him apart if a murder ever occurred in his peaceful town. They had occasional break-ins, assaults, thefts, and minor petty crime, but nothing like the rest of the country dealt with.

He was good at his job. Just not today.

He had already stopped by their church, St. Paul's Cathedral, and spoken to Father Benson, who didn't remember seeing the particular present that was slowly starting to burn a hole in his gut. Not that he dealt with every present, but like Elliot thought, Father Benson had remarked how old the paper looked and the delicacy of the red ribbon.

Elliot had even spoken to Eileen, who ran the front office in the cathedral. She handled each gift personally, not recognizing the gift, which spiked his annoyance level up the Richter scale to major. Of course, he swallowed any frustration with a kind thanks for her time. She thoughtfully suggested he check each church in the surrounding towns.

Like Mulberry, three other small towns clustered around the area before encountering a long stretch until reaching the first large city, St. Cloud. He had already checked Brighton and Melborne. That made Mason his last destination. As he took another turn, this time right, his chest constricted as a ray of sunlight struck his vision. The tightness slowly receded as the brightness enveloped the car. Was that hope swirling around?

A little bit of hope and a dash of luck would make the day even brighter. Otherwise, he'd have to assume someone left the gift on his porch from his own town. One horrible thought wouldn't leave.

Marybeth left it. The image of what she had in mind with the socks was a very disturbing one.

But that wily spark he had seen in his dad's eyes had to mean this gift came from one of the churches. Like a pirate looking for lost treasure, the mission would not end until he found the owner. Hell, he'd expand his search grid if he had to. No matter how many calming breaths or loosening of his limbs, the impulse to return the gift to its rightful owner coursed through his veins. It tingled in every nerve, refusing to stop. He'd solve this mystery before the day ended, or else.

Or else? Best not to think about that scary alternative.

He pulled into St. Mary's Cathedral parking lot and switched off the ignition. Gripping the steering wheel hard before releasing a small breath, he jumped out of the car as he clutched the present a little too tightly. Another breath escaped as he loosened his grip and climbed the four steps up to the front door of the church.

He didn't make it very far into the foyer when a friendly voice spoke from his left. "Good afternoon. How may I help you on this joyous day?"

Elliot turned toward the priest with a pasted smile. "Afternoon, Father. I'm Chief Duncan from Mulberry."

The priest stepped forward and shook his hand, his eyes grazing to the present gripped firmly in his other hand.

"I'm Father Preston. Welcome to Mason and to our wonderful church. I know Father Benson quite well. Do you go to church at St. Paul's?"

"Yes. I just saw Father Benson today. My dad also volunteers a lot, especially since he retired."

Geez, where had that useless piece of information come from? He didn't want to make small talk. He wanted to get rid of this present.

"What's your father's name? Duncan…that sounds familiar," Father Preston asked, his brows pleating in concentration.

"Gregory. He worked for the fire department in Mulberry for many years. He's always been active in the church."

Small sparks of heat ignited, the gift suddenly burning a hole in his hand. Enough with the small talk. And his own damn fault for starting it. Yet, polite manners stopped him from any kind of rude behavior.

"Ah, yes, Gregory Duncan. Wonderful man, your father. I saw him earlier today, actually. He looked very happy, like retirement is treating him well."

"Retirement has treated him well. I hate to take much more of your time, Father. I just have a quick question. Maybe a strange one, at that. This present," Elliot said, lifting it slightly, "do you know where it came from?"

Father Preston looked at the gift, his eyes transfixed. "I do know where it came from."

For the first time that day, the brightest smile emerged. Finally making some headway. "That's great to hear. Who donated it to the church? I don't know how it landed on my doorstep, but I'm here to correct that mistake and return it."

I can already imagine how that happened. Flexing his hand several times, a silent sigh blew away. His dad meant the best with his antics. Probably brought the gift home, unwittingly left it on the porch, and then let Elliot think it was for him since he had the nerve to open the damn gift. Why had he opened it?

"Oh, Chief Duncan, I can't just give out my parishioner's information. The presents are donated anonymously for a reason. It looks like you opened it. What was inside that you just can't accept?" Father Preston's smile never wavered as he spoke.

Was Father Preston playing him like his father had? Did everyone have it in for him this holiday season? What was so wrong with returning a gift that should go to a family who could actually use it?

"You misunderstood me. I'm sure there are a lot more families who could use this."

The gift hung in the air, waiting patiently for Father Preston to grab it, who just stared at him with a smile.

"We can sometimes never understand why things happen the way they do. Enjoy its contents. Merry Christmas, Chief."

"No, no, Father Preston, I insist. Take it, please." His hand would fall off before he dropped it and walked away.

"Have a blessed day, Chief Duncan." Father Preston snapped his fingers. "Oh, you know your father was supposed to drop off a donation box to the local diner,

Diana's Diner, for me. He offered to do it. Such a thoughtful gesture. Tara, the owner, she's kind enough to let people donate things to the church at the diner. He forgot to grab it before he left. Plus, they have excellent coffee. Would you be so kind to do it for me?"

How could he deny a priest's request? And his dad's memory. Should he be making a doctor appointment for him? His forgetfulness was increasing like the heat had in his house when the air conditioner broke down last summer.

"I'd be more than happy to do that for you. And thank you for your time, Father." Elliot offered a smile as Father Preston beamed with a grateful one and walked away to grab the donation box.

Elliot left the building with the blasted gift in one hand and the donation box in the other. Perhaps his problem was solved.

Donation box in one hand.

Gift in the other.

Put one inside the other.

Could he upset a priest? No doubt, Father Preston would notice and know exactly who put the gift in the box. Or did he just pass the gift off to someone else? Mulberry might be the better choice. Talk about a sin, upsetting a priest.

As he drove through town, the gift stared him down, its penetrating gaze making his fingers tighten on the wheel. Diana's Diner sat on the edge of town. Its quaint and inviting sign that offered the best home-cooked meals in the area brought a small grin. Home-cooked meals. His dad made some great meals, well, when he didn't burn it. But the effort to try to cook like his mom always lifted his soul.

Elliot almost grabbed the gift with the donation box. His

fingers still itched to toss it in. Instead, he stepped out of the truck and slammed the door before he changed his mind.

He stepped inside, the tiny bell hanging above the door ringing with happy vigor. A sweet voice floated from the kitchen. "Have a seat anywhere. I'll be right out."

Only one other customer, a straggly looking guy, occupied the space within the diner, sitting on the right side. That made the decision to sit on the left rather easy, facing the stranger with careful eyes. Maybe it was the cop in him, or maybe it was the way the guy looked dirty, unkempt, or just the fact he didn't know many people in this town. His eyes never strayed from the guy or the front door.

Elliot slid into a booth, set the box on the floor near his feet, and grabbed the menu stacked nicely in the rack pushed against the wall. He wasn't that hungry, but perhaps something would nab his attention. And coffee did sound good. Anything to settle the rattled nerves consuming his body.

Looking intently at the menu, his hand jerked as the same voice from earlier swirled around. This time, hearing the voice so close, it slid over him like a sweet caress. The smooth tone, the softness as each word left her mouth did something to Elliot that hadn't happened in, well, forever.

Another small strike to the lock on his heart.

Glancing up, his nerves rattled a little more. The shiny leather of the booth kept him anchored even as his body threatened to melt into a puddle of goo.

Pure beauty.

Strange, really, that such loveliness could be said as she wore a white shirt, a small red stain near the collar and a maroon apron tied around her waist that had seen better days. Her blonde hair was tied in a ponytail, long bangs covering her forehead that almost covered her eyes. It appeared she tried to curl them, but the longevity of the day had them flattening, taking normal residence over her bright brown eyes. Her simple, yet sweet smile lit up the room and a part of him as well.

"Did you decide what you want?" she asked again.

"Oh, sorry, I'm still looking. I hear the coffee's great." He turned away. The donation box. A great distraction to clear the embarrassment for gawking. "Father Preston asked me to drop this off. Where would you like me to put it?"

She glanced at the box, another gorgeous smile enriching her beauty. "I'll take it. He's always on top of things. The other box is almost full. It's so nice that everyone in town has such a generous heart, especially around the holidays."

His fingers grazed hers as she accepted the box. Tiny fireworks exploded. He had no words to her comment about the holidays. He didn't want to pretend that he liked the holidays as he did with everyone else. The light in her eyes when she spoke would probably dim if he put on an act.

A small frown appeared as she glanced at her hand. "Would you like a cup of coffee while you look over the menu?"

What was with the frown? Did she feel what he felt and not like it? Or was it his lack of response to her holiday comment? Maybe he should've pretended. The joy in her eyes and smile had dimmed anyway.

Lynn.

Just a quick peek at her nametag. Clearly, she was uncomfortable. No need to increase that by gawking even more.

"I'd love a cup, Lynn."

"I'll be right back."

Lynn quickly turned around, almost tripping. *Don't act like an idiot.* Just because a strange tingling sensation zapped her fingers when he touched her didn't mean anything. This was a test to see how horrible the day could proceed. How fast could she get the coffee and him out of the door, yet be polite and make a great tip?

Because any further tingles of delight would just make her clumsier. And if he used her name again, she just might melt into the floor like metal meeting fire. The way it rolled off his tongue like a sweet stroke across her body produced a shiver as she walked around the counter. One word and he made her into a blubbering mess.

And his penetrating stare. How bad did she truly look? A busy morning to a crazy lunch hour with several disasters. She never got this dirty. Of course, today, when a handsome man like that walks in, she has to look like she lost a paint war. That could be the only reasonable explanation why he hadn't looked away. The longer he stared, the temptation had swarmed like a raging tornado to brush her hair into a beautiful hairstyle, slap some makeup on, and even throw on a gorgeous dress. His eyes just had a way of sliding over her in a delicate, delicious manner.

She grabbed the coffeepot from the back counter, rolling her eyes as Jeremy whispered through the kitchen window, "He's hot. You look a little flustered. Give him another sweet smile and you'll make a helluva tip, darling. The way he's looking at you right now says so."

"Shh, Jeremy. That's just asking for trouble," Lynn whispered back.

"Well, the tip would be nice. But he's also looking at you like a man does when he really wants something for Christmas. Plus, I see a badge sticking out from under his coat. He's a lawman. How bad of a guy can he be?"

"That doesn't mean anything."

"Lynn, open your heart for once. If he asks you out, say yes. Or better yet, ask him out," Jeremy whispered, then backed away from the window with a parting wink.

Talk about increasing the nerves flying in every direction. Why would he put such thoughts in her head? Each step took complete concentration as she walked back to his table. A friendly smile appeared as she poured him a cup of coffee. Do the job. That's what gave her the tips she desperately needed. And don't spill a drop. Friendly or not, he could still stiff her if she didn't act like a professional.

"Anything look good?" she asked, as she stepped back for some much needed space. Plus, no spilling the coffee.

Would he really ask her out? Could she even ask him out? What was wrong with her? She wasn't going to ask him out. She knew nothing about this man other than he could ignite her body with a simple word. Her name. And her priority the next two weeks was to find three more gifts for her daughter, not to focus on a man. No matter how cute it was when his smile created two small dimples.

"Umm...pie. What do you suggest?"

"The apple pie is great. Or we have a wonderful mixed berry pie, created just for the holidays. Jeremy, our amazing cook, concocted it himself."

His face fell into a frown, dismissing his dimples with sudden ease. Why the sad look?

"Did I make the choice difficult? The apple pie is really great." *So is the berry pie.* God, it sat on the tip of her tongue to say it. Ugh! The choice *was* difficult. They both were really great.

His smile reappeared as if it never dissipated. "You really enjoy the holidays, don't you?"

Strange question.

"Christmas is a wonderful time of the year." A brow rose as she shifted her feet.

He looked pained for a brief second, so brief, she almost missed the flash of pain in his eyes. His smile never wavered once.

"I can hear the pleasure in your voice. It's nice."

Pleasure. Yeah, that was flowing just nicely, as his words —yet again—slid over her with a tender stroke.

But why the sad spark in his eyes? The smile stayed firmly in place, except the sadness couldn't be mistaken. Christmas was the one time of year that should lift a person up.

It could bring her down plenty of times, this morning a prime example. Just as swiftly, she removed those feelings like a broom to a dusty floor. Sweeping it with a brisk action as it flew home into the duster and right into the garbage can. Happy sensation back in its correct place.

"I love Christmas. Always have. Even when times get rough, I always will."

"It lights up your face so beautifully." He cleared his throat and looked down at the menu, tapping it gently. "Apple pie sounds great. I'll have a slice of that."

She walked away before more questions pelted his sad frame. And the compliment. He said she was beautiful. Another good reason to walk away. It didn't matter why he didn't like Christmas. Because that was clearly obvious. How could she even contemplate going out with a man that didn't like Christmas?

Wait! He didn't ask her out. One compliment and the assumptions emerged. He was just being polite.

Good. A nice tip was coming soon. Right?

ELLIOT SHIFTED in the booth as she walked away toward the counter again. The front door didn't matter. The strange looking man on the right seemed harmless. But removing her from his line of sight was simply impossible. She had the kind of legs that just begged a man to touch, to slide their hands all the way up to the spot they craved.

His pants tightened as he moved around the booth one more time. Inappropriate thoughts of a woman he barely knew. And she loved Christmas. Huge, blinking, warning sign right there. He had no time for a woman, especially one that enjoyed Christmas. How in the world could he continue faking his enjoyment for the holiday when her enthusiasm lit up the room?

Eat the apple pie. Almost like a contestant in a pie-eating contest. In and out of this diner. He had done his duty by dropping off the donation box. Made up for his father's forgetful memory. Seriously, he'd have to causally dig deeper into that. If his father needed to see a doctor, nothing would stop Elliot from forcing him to go. Losing his dad would be like the world ending by an asteroid.

Throwing a tired hand through his hair, he slowly dropped it as everything around him faded away—except one thing.

A bright red ribbon with glittery snowflakes sparkling like fresh dew on a cool spring day.

Holy shit!

The same ribbon that was on the gift outside in his vehicle. Was that a popular ribbon? Could you get that anywhere? Where had Lynn gotten it?

And damn, if it didn't look cute tied around her hair. Tied just as perfectly as the gift.

She strolled back to his table with a piece of pie and a gentle smile. Something about that smile gave a little strike to the lock on his heart.

The words to ask her about the gift stalled. That smile frightened him. Letting in any woman, especially this holiday spirited one would bring nothing good. She'd be offended he wanted to return her gift, if his assumptions about that bow were correct. A woman so happily infectious about Christmas wouldn't like her gift returned.

The coffee slid down his throat with a rancid flavor. How rude. Nobody had ever called him that. He couldn't return the gift to her. He'd never offend this gorgeous woman.

But he could still donate it somewhere else where she'd never know.

"Here you go. One slice of apple pie. Is the coffee as delicious as you were told?" she asked.

Almost choking as he took a sip, he tapped his chest to clear his throat. The earlier taste went down with guilt, but he couldn't deny it was good coffee. "Very. Thank you."

Another sweet grin from her. Damn that present. She turned around to walk away.

"Uh, Lynn, I have a question."

She stopped, her heart pounding so loudly, Jeremy in the kitchen could probably hear it. He couldn't possibly be asking her out. What would she say? Should she accept? What about Laura?

All ridiculous questions, of course. The near choking episode to her coffee question could only mean one thing.

The coffee wasn't that good. There went her tip. He probably wanted to know who made the coffee.

She had.

"Yep. How can I help?"

"I was thinking about donating a gift to the church...in Mulberry. That's where I live. I'm horrible at that sort of stuff. What would you suggest?"

The pounding slowed as her smile dipped a fraction. What an idiot! Of course, he wasn't going to ask for a date. And he clearly wasn't too concerned about the coffee. But a gift suggestion? His impression so far hadn't been very promising concerning Christmas. What in the world changed his mind? Or had she misinterpreted the sad look in his eyes?

Clearing her throat as a clammy hand slid down her apron, she lifted her smile back up. "Anything I'm sure you pick out will be excellent. Just giving is a wonderful thing."

Her smile never wavered, but the way his blue eyes held her transfixed, it wanted to. Every time he looked at her, it's as if he undressed her, sending tantalizing caresses across her skin.

Walk away! Get away from this man and his charming smile, his piercing eyes and calming voice.

"What would you give, you know, to help me with my gift?"

God, he was serious. But that sadness still lingered in the depths of his eyes. What put that pain there?

"Well, think of it this way. Give something that shows the Christmas spirit, that can last a lifetime if properly cared for, and can keep you warm at night. That's what I gave. I just love shopping for my daughter. I still haven't finished shopping for her. Not much time left." A heavy breath blew her bangs out of her eyes as the nerves still ran rampant throughout.

"How old is your daughter?"

"Seven. The light of my life."

"You still have plenty of time. Still two weeks to go."

"Yes, time. I'll leave you to your pie. Good luck with the gift." She took a step, then turned back toward the table and laid a white receipt with her usual thanks and holiday spirit attached. "The check. No rush."

He picked it up, his eyes accessing the check like he was about to interrogate a suspect. Was he really a cop? Did she mess up again? Maybe he didn't want the check already. Way to screw up a decent tip.

"What's this?" His finger pointed to her lovely message she always left.

May your holidays be ever bright.

"Just a bit of the Christmas spirit. It's a habit. I apologize if I offended you. I get the impression you don't like Christmas much."

He glanced away, a hint of red running up his neck, then looked back over with a grin that helped light up his eyes that had been sad moments before. "You're very perceptive. Most people don't notice. I'm not offended. I appreciate the gesture and your wonderful service."

She nodded as the relief swarmed back in. "I'll let you finish your pie."

So a good tip could still be had. She walked away before she ruined her chances. Not offended. How couldn't he be offended? He honestly admitted to not enjoying the holiday and she shoved it in his face.

With quick steps, she ducked inside the kitchen, ignoring Jeremy's kissing faces he made at her and stepped into the large walk-in freezer to cool down the heat he had ignited in her body. No amount of cold could tame the fire ignited by his sweet words and smooth voice that had stroked her body with delicious tingles.

Simple words had heated her up. What in the world would his actual touch do? His soft hands running over every inch of her skin. How soft would they be? So soft that they would take their time to caress every part of her body.

She fanned her face as she paced inside the freezer until all dangerous thoughts were clearly banished from her mind. Back to work. No more breaks, especially when she wasted a long one earlier trying to regain her composure from the crazy morning. More customers please. And a decent tip from the sweet man who disliked Christmas.

"You still look flushed," Jeremy said with a chuckle as she walked out of the freezer.

She promptly ignored him as she walked out of the kitchen. Her steps froze in place as the table moments before, occupied by the most intriguing man she had ever met, sat empty.

Tears pricked the corner of her eyes. Her chance at, God knows what, perhaps a date, gone. Yeah, right. He may have sparked a small flame of desire in her, but would a man that considerate and friendly really be unattached?

She approached the table. Money and a scrap of paper waited for her under the coffee cup.

Fifty dollars.

The coffee cup nearly fell over, as the shaking in her hand wouldn't stop. She wanted a nice tip, but fifty dollars? How could she accept this much money? She hadn't been that great of a waitress. No matter what he said, she touched a sore spot when she wrote that Christmas note on the receipt.

Her heart dropped to the floor as she read his note.

I had to leave. Thanks for the coffee and pie. I enjoyed them as much as I enjoyed talking to you. I'm still having trouble thinking of a gift idea. I hope you come up with a great idea for me. Until I see you again, Lynn, I'll be thinking of you.

Elliot Duncan

3

Okay, four clues to help solve her problem.

He's from Mulberry, spoken from the man himself.

He's a cop, observed by Jeremy. She trusted his opinion.

His name is Elliot Duncan, written by his hand.

He has a smile that creates two tiny dimples that are simply adorable and a smooth voice that makes her heart beat with excitement.

Well, that last one really wasn't a clue. Or even a good reason why she was in her car driving to Mulberry with the start of a decent snowfall.

But she had to return the fifty dollars to Elliot. No negotiations. Way too much money. She hadn't provided *that* great of service either.

Lynn reached for the volume control, turning it up a notch to let the music distract her mind. The wondrous melody drifted throughout the car as the white glistening snow fell down in a graceful wave.

Those eyes. Blue as the shimmering lakes that graced

Minnesota. Amazing what one simple gaze from that man could do to her.

Ugh! Stop thinking about him. Repeat goal one more time. Return the money and that's it. Nothing more.

A soothing sigh slowly floated out as she pulled into a parking spot not far from the doors to the police station. Mission soon to be accomplished and then she could focus on how to make more money than ever before to buy the rest of Laura's presents. Nothing to it.

Tiny laughter shifted around the swirling cold. Yeah, right! Talk about a challenge.

With quick long strides, as long of strides her short legs could give, she headed for the front door. The biting cold and bustling snow didn't impede one step. Not that she would've let it. Nothing would stop her from this goal.

Her feet did a one eighty to turn around as the idea to confront him suddenly terrified her. Just as swiftly, she knocked out that crazy notion and continued around to her normal direction. To anyone watching, it probably looked like she just twirled in a complete circle, dancing in the beautiful snow.

Yeah, she'd go with that excuse if anyone dared to stop and ask her. Playing in the snow was fun. She and Laura would have to pull out the snow gear once a decent blanket of snow landed on the ground. By the looks of it, they'd have it in no time.

With jerky steps, she approached the door as it swung open, nearly clocking her in the face. She started to tumble backwards to avoid contact, as her shoes that had seen better days, slid on the sidewalk. A strong hand grasped her arm, stopping the treacherous downward fall.

"Geez, I'm so sorry. I can't believe I almost knocked you down. It's a surprise to see you again so soon, Lynn."

Her eyes slowly lifted from the white packed ground to the face of the man she had been trying to forget.

Why was she trying to forget him again? Even with gloves covering his hands, the tiny sparks of desire shocked her very core.

"Elliot. Just the man I was looking for. No apologies necessary." She politely extracted her arm from his grip and took a step back. Space was good. Lots of space.

A warm smile produced the dimples she just loved. "You were looking for me? Should I be worried or excited?"

Laughing, she tugged on her purse to dig for the fifty. "That depends. And this by no means is meant as an insult or my ungratefulness. It was truly a kind gesture."

Elliot frowned. "You have me confused. Which makes me lean towards worried."

"You were thoughtful with the tip you left, but I can't accept this much money. While I appreciate the kind gesture, it's just too much. I basically insulted you by throwing Christmas in your face and the coffee didn't seem as good as you probably like it. Here you go."

Like the lead on a fishing line, her hand dangled in the air wanting to fall in despair as she waited for him to take it. Why wasn't he taking it? And that frown. How much lower could he possibly get it?

"I already told you I wasn't offended. And the coffee was great. You deserved every bit of that tip I left. Not to mention I left abruptly. Please keep it."

His roughened glove clutched her hand, pushing it toward her purse. Putting on gloves of her own would've been very wise. Perhaps that would've helped to create a better barrier at his electrifying touch.

"I insist." She halted her hand to go any further, forming a small tug of war with him.

Elliot lightly laughed as he let go of her hand. "I don't wish to fight with you, Lynn. That's the furthest thing from my mind."

His sweet, yet masculine laugh, almost made her knees buckle. What was front and center in his mind, then?

"Good. Here you go."

Ignoring her, he gestured down the sidewalk. "I just had a helluva afternoon. Care to join me for a cup of coffee? I'll show you just how good yours really was. The coffee this way can't even compare."

Mimicking his frown from earlier, her fist clenched the fifty. "I think you're trying to appease me so I forget about the money. I don't forget things, Elliot."

"Maybe I just want to enjoy your company. Is that so hard to believe?"

"Take the money and I'll believe you."

"Follow me and I'll consider it."

She couldn't resist that lovable smile of his or the way his eyes glittered with anticipation. "Fine. One cup. And you will take the money."

"We'll see. I'm not officially convinced yet." He chuckled as he placed a hand on her back briefly, then let it fall as they made their way down the sidewalk.

A few minutes later, settled in a booth out of the harsh cold, Lynn took a sip of the coffee. Scrunching her face, the black sludge slid down her throat with an acrid taste.

"Told you it wasn't as good as yours." His eyes twinkled as he took a sip.

"Somehow I think you still come here a lot, don't you?"

"Theresa tries. It doesn't taste the same on any given day. I have faith one of these days she'll get it right."

With a laugh, she took another sip. Nope, still tasted disgusting. "You're a very kind man, Elliot."

"And you have a beautiful laugh." He cleared his throat. "You don't like it when I compliment you, do you?"

God, didn't she hide her wince well enough? "Just surprising, that's all."

"Why would that surprise you?"

"Why don't you like Christmas?"

Leaning back in the booth, his eyes clouded over with sadness. "Avoiding a question with a question. Very smooth."

Why did she keep bringing up Christmas? That sadness of his brought her down every time. "Avoiding a question with a statement of the obvious."

The light brightened in his eyes once again. "How did you find me? I'm very impressed."

"You provided me with all very good clues. Your name, where you live, and I thought I saw a badge clipped to your belt." A total lie, that last one, but Jeremy saw it. That was close enough to the truth.

"Damn, you'd make a good cop. It also makes me think I need to be a little less forthcoming with my information to strangers." His brow lifted with amusement.

"Are we strangers, Elliot?"

He leaned forward, his hand twitching as if he wanted to reach out toward her. "Not any more. Friends?"

She lifted her cup, smiling above the rim. "Friends sounds nice. As your friend, I insist you take that fifty back."

He laughed as he shook his head. "I haven't reached that point yet where I want to take it back. I might need food to mull it over some more."

Oh, Elliot. His hints weren't that subtle. He was totally flirting with her. She couldn't help but fall under his charm.

"Chief, there you are."

Lynn turned around to see a man dressed in a police

uniform gesture to Elliot. She glanced toward Elliot as he stood up from the booth. With his gorgeous smile, he said, "I'll be right back. Food, then?"

She flashed him a smile.

※

WALKING AWAY from Lynn was a lot harder than he imagined. It wasn't like he wouldn't be joining her back in the booth. Or would he? *Please don't let this take me away from her.* That already happened once today, upsetting him more than he realized. He couldn't be sure how much longer he could throw tidbits out to her that he wanted her company and not just ask for her number. This wasn't high school. He shouldn't be acting like a geeky teenager afraid to ask out his crush.

"What's up, Officer Crowl?"

"Roads are starting to get bad. My shift's over in an hour, but if you need me to stay on..." He hesitated as he shifted his feet. "I know the overtime doesn't always get approved."

"How about on-call? If I need you, you'll be the first person I contact."

"Thanks, Chief. Appreciate it."

"No problem."

The door swished closed as Officer Crowl walked out. Elliot's heart dipped that he couldn't help him out. He knew exactly why he wanted to work. Sometimes working drowned out the pain. Losing his fiancé four months ago, he knew how much pain Officer Crowl had inside.

Elliot walked back to the table, offering Lynn a small smile. What were the odds she wouldn't bring up the money again? Pretty low. She seemed very determined.

So was he. That blasted gift of hers was still in his car

with a twenty-dollar bill just wasting away. Not one to be judgmental, but he didn't think money grew on trees for Lynn. She needed that money, especially the fifty she insisted he take back. Now, he just had to convince her to keep it.

"Sorry about that. My job can get crazy sometimes."

"I understand. That snow really looks like it's coming down. I should go. It was nice talking to you, Elliot." She smiled brightly at him as she stood up from the booth.

He just sat down and she was running from him. There was no mistaking that. How had he scared her? Probably the damn food suggestion. He should've toned it down a bit.

Then he glanced out the window. Nothing but a winter wonderland stared back. The snow *was* coming down heavily. Perhaps that made her forget about the money. And he wasn't going to mention it.

"Please drive safe, Lynn. Maybe you should ca—"

"Have a good night. Drive safe as well." She cut him off and rushed out of the café before he could utter one protest.

He almost accomplished his goal. Getting her number. And she shut him down. Very well, actually. Lynn had a six sense of things, apparently. She had to have known he was about to say, "Call me when you get home."

Damn!

Two dollars near her coffee cup drew his attention.

She didn't even let him pay for her coffee. Shaking his head, he grabbed his cup for another sip of the dreadful coffee that he'd gotten quite used to. Perhaps he supported Theresa's habit a little too much. His taste buds were losing their senses.

The cup nearly slipped from his grasp as more green hit his eyes.

A fifty-dollar bill.

She tucked the fifty under his cup so neatly there wasn't a chance he would see it until he picked it up. Sneaky, sneaky woman.

Very impressive. A smile grew.

Elliot paid for his coffee and walked outside to the sharp, cold snow blowing around. It didn't seem to be settling down at all.

Lynn's beautiful face flashed before him. How would he know if she made it home? He didn't even know where her home was. He knew where she worked. Would one of her co-workers give him her number? Not likely. But perhaps they would call her for him to make sure she got home safely.

She only drove to Mulberry in this weather to return his money that he wanted her to have. He still did.

He slammed his truck door closed and blasted the heat as soon as the engine roared to life. What the hell was he doing? Driving in this weather on a mission that would likely not end in his favor was just pure craziness.

Regardless, he turned toward Mason and a diner that would hopefully guide him back to Lynn. Another hammer to that lock around his heart. The lock would fall away pretty soon if he didn't stop these crazy impulses.

Maybe that wouldn't be such a bad thing. Not with Lynn as the one chipping away at it.

4

Lynn leaned forward, gripped the steering wheel hard, and sat so close to the wheel that her chin nearly rested on top of it. Making out anything with the snow pouring down like a gushing waterfall was almost impossible. The roads were blanketed in white, the snow packed hard to the road. It appeared the plows had already come through this area, but they needed to come through again. The little they plowed hadn't made a difference.

Why had her stubborn mind insisted on returning that fifty today? The snow started falling before she even left the diner. She knew better than to make this drive while it snowed. Now look at the predicament she put herself in.

She made fifty dollars today. Fifty! She never made that much from one person. Maybe that's why she couldn't find it in herself to keep it. Keeping it had felt wrong.

What did he say when he found it tucked under his cup? Such a chicken not staying to find out. Most likely, he would've tried putting it back in her hands. More touching.

And touching from him was bad. Very, very bad. The

way her body lit up with flaming heat of desire was more than she could handle. His note, she already read it at least a hundred times back at the diner before she left. Almost like a love note the way she kept pulling it out of her pocket and cherishing every word he wrote. In person, he still said the sweetest things.

You have a beautiful laugh.

Why did he have to be so sweet? It made it more difficult to walk away. Using the snow as an excuse, a very good one, still didn't make it any easier. Would he still come back to the diner and see her? Just thinking about a next possible encounter had her shivering with anticipation.

Easing her foot from the gas, she slowed her pace even more when the car lurched slightly to the right. Damn slick roads. Why did it have to snow?

Thank goodness for such wonderful friends. Debbie, who lived a street over, graciously said she would watch Laura while she ran some errands. Lynn never specified what those errands would be and Debbie didn't ask. Telling her she was trying to locate a man to return fifty dollars didn't seem like the brightest idea. She could already imagine Debbie's mischievous smile at her tracking down a man for any reason. Lynn rarely dated. Things like this were so unlike her.

That made her pause. God, had she tracked him down to return the fifty or because she wanted to see him again so soon?

Ridiculous! She didn't need a man in her life. She would never do anything so silly. It was to return the money. End of story.

The car suddenly jerked, slamming her violently in the seat. A ringing sensation rippled throughout her ears, blocking out any coherent thought. Her hands still clutched the wheel as a sharp pain radiated from her head, down her spine, and to the tips of her toes.

Slowly, she removed her hands and lifted one toward her forehead. An icky substance smothered her fingers. Those gloves would've come in handy again. Feeling the blood didn't help soothe any nerves. But why should any part of the day go right? She had forgotten her winter gloves on the kitchen counter this morning. Now her stomach wanted to lurch from the blood on her hands.

Blinking a few times, confusion still swirled around the car like the white snow billowing outside. The ringing intensified.

"Shit, Lynn, what did you do?" she muttered as a bit of her strength renewed. Grabbing her purse from the passenger seat, she started to rummage for a tissue.

Great! A crumpled up wad of tissues. Who knew how long this had been sitting in the bottom of her purse? Beggars couldn't be choosers. Stifling a painful groan, she pressed it lightly to the cut on her forehead.

Looking out each window, nothing but the dark night and winter wonderland reflected back. A very fitting end to a frustrating day. Running her car off the road into the ditch ended it just nicely. *God, please be in the ditch*. It wasn't exactly clear with everything looking like one big field of white snow. That's what happened when the mind wandered. Or blaming the snow would be good, too. That actually made her pride feel a little better.

With her car suddenly shutting off from the impact, the cold air seeped in rather quickly. Or was that shock? Either way, the car needed to start. Rubbing her hands together for luck, because she really needed her car to start, she twisted the key.

Nothing but silence answered back.

"No, no, no, you piece of shit, start, damn it." Lynn blew out a breath, squeezed her eyes shut tightly before opening them and rubbed her hands delicately over the wheel. "I'm so sorry, my beautiful car. I didn't mean those nasty words. Please, please, start for me. I need you to work. I can't afford to fix you. Even if it wasn't Christmas, and I didn't need to finish shopping for Laura, I don't have the money to replace you. I also need to pay the rent. Start for me, beautiful."

Another large breath released as she turned the key again.

Nothing.

She leaned her head against the steering wheel, cursing loudly as the pain from her cut increased with tiny pinpricks rushing down her body.

Oh, that's right. An injury she couldn't afford to have. Completely unaware she had dropped the rumpled tissue, she picked it up from her lap, cringing at how blood-soaked it had already become. Stitches were the last thing she needed. Her stomach lurched again.

This couldn't be the only tissues she had. Digging through her purse again, her hands clenched fiercely when she couldn't find any other tissues lingering in the depths. Throwing her purse to the ground wouldn't solve anything. No need to panic yet.

Reaching over to the glove box, the seatbelt jerked, impeding her new mission. Wincing with pain, she rubbed her chest and the probable bruise she received from the seatbelt when her car slammed into the ditch.

She unbuckled her belt and reached again for the glove box. A happy sigh escaped when a small bag of tissues graced the small space. She grabbed the entire thing, pulled some out and pressed it gently to her forehead.

Now what? Her car wouldn't start and the cold was

already starting to weave its way down her spine and settle with permanency. It would only get worse if she couldn't get her car started. Outside definitely held the cold blowing snow that would freeze her without much effort. Screwed either way.

What were the odds of another crazy person driving in this mess and finding her stuck on the side of the ride?

Crap! Glancing frantically out the window, the churning wind made it impossible to tell where her car landed. How much worse could it get?

❄

OKAY, as the chief of police, Elliot knew better. Heading out into the snow that looked more and more like a soon-to-be blizzard, maybe not such a good idea. But what did that tell him about Lynn? A cop for many years, he was accustomed to this kind of weather, venturing out to help stranded people or responding to traffic accidents where a simple push got the car unstuck. Or the really dreadful traffic accidents that no one could erase from their mind, even though they tried as hard as they could. Death was a way of life. It didn't mean he, or any of his officers, wanted to deal with it.

But Lynn. Not likely she would be used to this sort of weather.

Did she make it home alright? Would the diner still be open? The diner where they enjoyed the coffee would already be closed. That's what happened in small towns when the weather became like this. Regardless of the consequences to himself, he had to at least try and make sure Lynn made it home okay. The thought otherwise wouldn't be sensible to contemplate, especially now when he needed his full concentration.

Why did she have to return the fifty anyway? It was nothing more than a kind gesture on his part, not to mention he had nothing less than a fifty in his wallet at the time. Plus, being Christmas and all, why not receive an extra large tip. She looked like she deserved it no matter what she thought about her service skills.

The steering wheel jerked, almost veering off the road. Shit! Him, thinking of Christmas in such a nice way. He hadn't thought that way in a long time. Just look at what this woman was doing to him. Making him think about Christmas in a positive way.

Of course, the sweet way her face lit up talking about the holidays, he couldn't help but smile right along with her. She made him want to like Christmas again. Strange, considering he couldn't even find the joy when his dad tried. But that lingering sadness still weighed down his heart. One day around a beautiful woman, who could make Christmas sound splendid, didn't erase all of the painful memories.

Leaning forward some, he tried to focus on the road instead of his wandering thoughts. The weather appeared to be getting worse by the minute. Thank goodness, that Mason was only a twenty-minute drive from Mulberry. With the current conditions, imagining how much worse it would be with a longer drive wouldn't be wise.

A quick glance to the dashboard showed he was only going twenty in a forty-five mile-a-hour zone. Nobody could say he was speeding, but with the snow impeding his view, it could be considered too fast. The plows didn't look like they reached this stretch of the road yet. Or maybe they had and the snow was just beating down too fast for anything to make a difference. On this road, they needed to be constantly plowed back and forth. Nothing stretched on the sides of this road between

Mason and Mulberry but green fields and wide-open spaces. That made everything worse. It all blended as one.

He let his foot off the gas a little more, praying that Lynn made it home safely. Guilt was starting to weave its way in. If he would've never left such a large tip that she felt obligated to return, she never would've made the drive to Mulberry to find him.

Gazing toward his right, a car nestled precariously on the side of the road. He couldn't tell if anyone was still inside, but the cop in him had him pulling over to make sure. Checking the rearview mirror before stepping outside, he jogged over to the car as he kept his head down from the pelting snow.

A lone figure sat in the driver's seat. He knocked gently on the window and almost lost his balance when the last person he expected to see turned toward the noise.

Lynn.

It was his fault she had been on the road to begin with.

His heart started pounding madly as she rolled her window halfway down.

"Lynn! Are you alright? You're bleeding." Elliot pulled on the door handle, except it wouldn't budge. "Open the door so I can look at that gash."

"Elliot?" Lynn gaped at him, the surprise clear as a sunny day to see him standing outside her car.

"The door, Lynn. Unlock it for me."

Resisting the urge to reach through the window and unlock it himself took more restraint than he could ever imagine. Worry pelted him like the cold snow slapped his face, creating a turbulent sea in the pit of his stomach. So many worst-case scenarios flashed before him. What would've happened if he never decided to follow her home?

What if he hadn't seen the car perched on the side of the road? How much blood had she lost so far?

God, seeing the ones he cared about in pain tore him up inside. He cared about Lynn, no doubt about that.

Where had this sudden protective need to care for her come from? Perhaps from all those little hammers to the lock on his heart. She had managed to weasel her way in without much effort.

Damn! He wanted a real merry Christmas for once —with her.

"Lynn, you're scaring me. Open the door, please."

Finally snapping out of her shock, she hit the unlock button. That beautiful sound was like music to his ears, not even a millisecond went by as he whipped open the door and crouched down in front of her. Without hesitating, he pulled her hand away and cradled her face.

A nasty gash on her forehead was bleeding steadily.

"Shit, that's pretty deep. You might need stitches. What happened?"

She continued to stare at him with a glazed look, igniting his fear further into his bones.

"Lynn, talk to me. Are you injured somewhere else I can't see?"

"I'm sorry, Elliot. I'm...my head hurts. I don't know what happened. I was driving, then I was slamming into the steering wheel."

"Come on. Let's get you in my truck and I'll drive you to the hospital in Mulberry. I don't think Mason has one."

"No, they don't, but I don't need—"

"We're not arguing about this. You need stitches," he said firmly, brushing a soft hand across her cheek. "Please, don't argue. Do you need to grab anything? Your car isn't going anywhere tonight with the way the snow's coming down."

She shook her head, wincing. "Just my purse."

She pulled away from him, yanked her keys from the ignition and threw them into her purse. Elliot rolled her window back up and hit the lock switch. She slowly faced him again. He gave her the most reassuring smile he could manage. His concern was too massive to grace her with an honest-to-goodness smile she deserved.

Backing up a few steps as a wetness started to flood his shoes, she almost fell face first into the snow. "Let me help you. Wait for me, Lynn." Looping an arm around her waist, he held her firmly as more coldness seeped into his body. She was like an icicle.

His footsteps wobbled through the snow as he helped her out of the ditch and into his truck. And those shaky footsteps weren't just from the snow making it difficult to walk.

Heat. Lynn needed lots of heat. His fingers shook like the leaves on a tree on a windy day as he blasted the heat and then opened the middle compartment between his seat and hers, grabbing some tissues. "Here, press this to that gash. I'll get you there in no time."

"Where were you going in this weather?" She pressed the tissues to her head, wincing in pain as the tissues soaked rather quickly.

Offering another sweet smile, he said, "Would you believe me if I said I wanted another cup of that delicious coffee? Theresa's just didn't hit the spot."

She chuckled. "I don't know. I don't think our coffee is *that* delicious."

"Trust me, it is." He paused, then stole another sly glance before focusing his attention to the road. "I was worried about you. I wanted to make sure you got home okay."

"And how were you going to manage to do that? You don't know where I live."

"I wasn't really sure. Call it an impulse when you left so quickly. You forgot your tip as well. I wanted to give that back."

Focusing on the road was the top priority, but he couldn't help risking another glance at her when she remained silent. Her lips were pressed tightly together with her eyes straight ahead.

"Everyone deserves a decent tip once in a while. You gave the entire thing back. Now it's like I gave you nothing. At least let me give you something. And I wanted to pay for your coffee at the diner."

She sighed heavily. "You said earlier you had a crazy afternoon. What happened?"

"Wow, dodging me again. You seem to be really good at that." Chuckling, he decided to let her have her way. For the moment, anyway.

"There was an incident at the local bar, one of my buddies, Fred, was getting into it with another customer. The bartender, another good friend of mine, he called me. He didn't want Fred to get arrested, but he needed him to calm down and get him out of the bar. He's been having a tough time and getting arrested wouldn't help him any."

"I thought I heard that officer call you chief."

"I'm the chief of police. I get calls all the time to deal with a lot of small stuff. But really, if I can solve an issue without making an arrest, I call that a good thing."

"You sound like you love your job."

"I do, most days. Do you enjoy your job?"

She shrugged, dropping her hand as the tissues started

to become too saturated to hold against her forehead any longer.

"Here. You have to keep pressure on that wound. Just throw those on the floor," he said, holding out the remaining tissues to her. "Honestly, Lynn, just toss those on the floor. It's not a big deal. We'll be there soon."

She smiled weakly, following his instructions. "Why is your friend having a hard time?"

"He's going through a nasty divorce, custody battle, the whole nine yards. I tried to tell him getting drunk and getting into a fight wasn't going to help him. He left the bar peacefully, but I'm not really sure he heard my words."

"It was nice of you to help the way you did. I'm sure he would've gotten arrested anywhere else acting like that."

He shook his head. "You're probably right. He just wants to see his kids and she won't let him. He needs to start keeping it at home because there might come a time when I won't be there to save him."

"I can't imagine never seeing Laura. That's just sad to think about."

Elliot didn't doubt that. Her eyes immediately shined with love whenever she spoke about her daughter. Just one more thing to like about her. The list kept getting longer and longer, except that damn tip wedging its way between them.

"Did you call her? Or your husband, or boyfriend, that you had an accident?"

What a dumb question. Did he even want to hear the answer to his last question? Easiest way to put that lock firmly back in place if she would say, "Yes, I called my wonderful husband. He's so worried about me."

"You'll probably think me silly, and ridiculously outdated, but I don't own a cell phone. I'm not really sure I want to call her yet. She'll just worry."

A groan wanted to escape. Well, that didn't answer both of his questions. Did that mean she had a man waiting at home for her? Maybe that's why she fled so fast from the diner. He felt like a teenager back in high school, worrying tirelessly that his crush liked someone else.

"So, no one else but your daughter that you would need to call?"

She turned her head slightly, looking at him with a delightful smile. "No, nobody else. A good friend of mine is watching her for me. Her father died a long time ago, in a car crash, actually. Another reason I don't care to tell her what happened. Anybody waiting at home for you?"

Slowing the car down to give her a good long look and not run off the road, he turned toward her. "No, nobody. Unless you count my dad."

"He could be worried. A parent never stops worrying no matter how old you get."

"True enough. When you want to use my phone and call your daughter, you're more than welcome to."

"Thank you, Elliot. That's very kind of you."

"And while you're at it, add your number in my contacts before you hand my phone back."

There. He finally said it. The words were lame even to his own ears. What a lousy pickup line!

She laughed a gentle, wonderful sound that briefly made his nerves start to relax. "Very smooth, Elliot. Are you asking me out?"

"Well, considering I wanted to ask you for your number before you rushed out on me, then yes, I am." He grinned, enjoying another velvety laugh that left her lips.

"Well, if I use your phone, I'll be sure to add it."

He flickered another look, his heart filling with pleasure as a shy, flirty smile graced her beautiful face. Just as swiftly, concern swooped in by the look of how blood-soaked the tissues were still getting. "Then I'll make sure you definitely use it before the night's over."

The rest of the ride continued with small talk, her voice getting tired by the minute. Fifteen minutes later, he pulled into the emergency room parking lot.

With frenzied movements, he hopped out. The drive had taken longer than he liked. Lynn's coloring concerned him. He rounded the front of the truck and nearly slipped on the snow-covered ground. The passenger door started to open. "Wait for me to help you, Lynn. It's slippery out here."

Before she could respond, her feet slipped on the soft ground, propelling her downward. Elliot barely reached her time and scooped her up into his warm embrace. When her eyes refused to open after repeated attempts of calling her name, the worry he had from the beginning turned into a full-blown meltdown.

5

Elliot's panic spiraled as Lynn refused to open her beautiful eyes. What other injuries had she sustained? He stood frozen, everything paralyzing him. He never panicked in such a manner, and yet, here he stood panicking like a deer in headlights.

Her soft moan finally snapped him out of his trance. "I got you, Lynn. Everything's going to be okay."

Walking toward the emergency room doors with quick, yet careful steps, he knew he said those words more for his benefit than hers. Everything had to be okay. She needed to walk out of this hospital on her own two feet, not with him carrying her out in his arms or wheeled in a chair, or worse yet, not even walking out of the hospital at all.

Stop! Thinking those kinds of thoughts didn't help. But every time he passed the hospital, his heart always paused a beat or two. He spent too many days in this hospital watching his mother slowly wither away as the cancer took her from him. Of course, this wasn't the first time he had been back to the hospital. Nope. He had to venture back when his dad had his heart attack.

Definitely not a happy place for him. Being here was the last thing he wanted, but he wouldn't leave Lynn's side until she left the hospital. And she would leave. It was just a small gash.

"Chief Duncan, who do you have there?" Erin, one of the nicest nurses he knew in the hospital, said from behind the front counter.

She circled the counter as he responded, "Lynn Carpenter from Mason. Car accident. She has a nasty gash on her forehead and she slipped getting out of the truck. I managed to catch her before she hit the ground, but she hasn't opened her eyes since, just moans here and there."

Erin could obviously hear the alarm in his voice because she placed a calming hand on his shoulder. "She's in good hands here. Let's get her to exam room 5. Dr. Pearson is working tonight. She might have a concussion."

Elliot followed Erin and gently placed Lynn on the bed as Erin dashed to get Dr. Pearson. Before she came back with the doctor, Lynn finally opened her eyes, confusion marring her features. "What happened? Where am I?"

"You blacked out on me. Fell out of the truck. Next time wait for me. You have this thing about wanting to do everything yourself."

"Do I? I hadn't noticed." A weak smile emerged at the same time her eyes fluttered closed.

Elliot brushed a hand over her soft cheek as he used his other hand to grasp her hand in a tight grip. "The doctor will be right in."

"You've been so kind tonight."

"Ah, yes, Elliot is the supreme gentleman. It's still a wonder why he's single. Try not to let anyone else know you're here. I'll have all the available women, nurses and patients included, flocking to your side," Dr. Pearson said, curling his lips into a devilish grin.

"Oh, come on, Doc, we all know they would secretly be flocking to you, pretending they're here for me." Elliot chuckled. The man knew Elliot well, especially with the many visits to his mother. He knew the anxiety Elliot was probably experiencing, yet trying to hide it, and hiding it well, as Lynn hadn't commented on the tapping of his agitated foot or the slight tremor in his hand that held hers.

"You bashful man, I already saw Erin's red cheeks as I walked away." Dr. Pearson winked, walking to the other side of Lynn. "What happened here, my dear?"

"I hit my head on the steering wheel crashing my car in the ditch," Lynn mumbled between biting slashes of pain as Dr. Pearson examined her head.

"She blacked out outside as well," Elliot added.

Dr. Pearson looked over at Elliot, the concern clear in his eyes. Could he hear the fear in his voice as Erin had? Quashing that fear seemed impossible. At least, not until they both walked out of the hospital.

"Perhaps you should wait out in the waiting room, Elliot."

What if something happened if he left the room? "Well, I—"

"I'd like him to stay, please," Lynn interrupted.

Dr. Pearson nodded at Lynn, then glanced at Elliot with a look that conveyed he calm down.

Elliot tried to obey as he held Lynn's hand while Dr. Pearson stitched the nasty gash on her head, but the shaking in his hand and the tapping of his foot didn't seize even for a moment.

※

TEN STITCHES LATER, no more blood trickled down her face. Not a feeling she wanted to experience again anytime soon. While Dr. Pearson conducted several more tests, asking questions, and examining the rest of her body to make sure she suffered no other injuries, she clung to Elliot's hand. She had a small bruise forming from her seatbelt, but nothing to worry about, according to Dr. Pearson.

So, she wouldn't worry about it. It was easy to do that while Elliot held her hand. He offered comfort. Acted as her protector. Made her completely forget why she shouldn't worry.

Such a strange feeling she hadn't felt in a long time. There were moments when Dr. Pearson had asked her a question and she couldn't formulate any words as Elliot's soft hands gripped her with such fierceness. She could now confirm they were soft. His hands were warm and soothing. Her head almost didn't hurt when he touched her.

Didn't she tell herself no more touching?

Well, she was completely wrong. His touch did wonders.

Was her touch doing something to him as well?

She swore she heard panic in his voice on the ride to the hospital. And the concern. So dominant it had shocked her. He had been truly concerned. More than she ever thought possible. They barely knew each other.

She didn't doubt it anymore because, even as he tried to hide it, she could feel the small vibrations from his hand. His nerves were shining clear as day. Yet, there was a tenderness that made her heart melt inside.

Where was a freezer when she needed it to cool down from his heated touch? If that would even help. Not even the cold snow blowing outside could probably cool her down.

"You have several symptoms of a concussion. You can't be alone for the next twenty-four hours nor do I want you sleeping more than two hours at a time. I can admit you overnight for—"

"Oh, no, Doctor, I can't do that. I feel fine, really," Lynn exclaimed, cutting off the doctor without caring how rude it sounded.

Absolutely not. Staying overnight was the last thing she could do. Laura needed her. Debbie was probably wondering why she hadn't returned home yet. She needed to call her.

"Maybe you feel fine, but that doesn't mean you are. I don't like that you blacked out in the parking lot. You can't take a concussion lightly, Ms. Carpenter," Dr. Pearson said with sympathy, but also with firmness.

"I have a daughter. I just can't stay here, the mon—I can't stay here." Shivers rushed through as the predicament before her loomed with despair. She honestly felt fine. Well, besides the raging headache, the slight dizziness, and a little bit nauseated, she felt absolutely fine.

"Do you have someone to stay with you, Lynn, wake you up every couple of hours just to make sure you're alright? I'm sure it's okay to go home if that's the case, right, Doc?" Elliot asked.

Another good reason to have him by her side. He could do all the thinking of great ideas for her.

"That would be fine, but it's imperative that someone watches you. If any of your symptoms get worse, you need to come back immediately. Who will stay with you?"

Lynn stared at Dr. Pearson. By the powerful look in his eyes, he wouldn't just accept any old answer. He would smell a lie a mile away. Who would watch over her?

She could ask Debbie, knowing she wouldn't hesitate to help, but that didn't sit well with her. Debbie worked at the local grocery store, always the one who opened the bakery first thing in the morning. She had to be to work by 6 AM. That wouldn't be a full twenty-four hours.

The longer she delayed an answer, the more Dr. Pearson would know she's lying.

"I think...ah, I can't stay here," Lynn said desperately.

"Well, I'm almost not sure you can drive back to Mason in this horrible weather. The snow isn't planning to stop any time soon. You've already been injured once in this weather, I don't want to see you again for another more serious injury," Dr. Pearson said.

"That's very true, Doc. Lynn, can your daughter stay overnight with your babysitter? My house isn't too far from the hospital. You can stay with me and I'll bring you back home tomorrow. Problem solved, all around," Elliot said with such compassion she almost blurted yes immediately.

"I have to work tomorrow. I have to be there by eight. I need to work."

While she wanted desperately to accept his suggestion, she couldn't miss a day of work, or leave Laura at Debbie's. Not that Laura never had a sleepover at Debbie's, because she had. Loved spending time over at Debbie's, actually. She was like an aunt to her. Debbie would say yes in a heartbeat, especially if she knew the state Lynn was in.

Elliot squeezed her hand, his warmth and thoughtfulness slipping further into her heart. "Lynn, I get the feeling money is tight with you. But, please, think of your health. You can't work tomorrow regardless of where you go. You need at least a day of rest to make sure you have no more signs of a concussion."

"Elliot is right, my dear," Dr. Pearson said quietly.

"You don't understand, Elliot. I—"

"I do. I understand." He leaned closer, delicately whispering in her ear, "I still owe you a decent tip."

He moved away as his eyes sparkled with gentleness. "I promise you can go back the next day, and I'll be damn sure to come and order a cup of that delicious coffee."

He smiled with charm that almost said he would leave another fifty. Not that she would accept that one, or the first one he still insisted she take back. But that smile almost managed to calm her worries.

"I can't accept your money like that." The sweetness in this wonderful man seemed too good to be true as she grinned back. "The coffee isn't that delicious."

"I don't know why you don't believe me." His smile beamed a little brighter, hitting a spot in her heart that she thought she'd never open again for a man.

"You're making me a believer. Where do I get a cup of this delicious coffee?" Dr. Pearson asked with a grin.

"Diana's Diner in Mason. I highly recommend it," Elliot replied.

"Oh, stop, you two." Lynn laughed, despite the extreme worry plaguing her. "The snow is pretty bad, isn't it?"

"Yes, it is. I'll bring you home if you really want me to, but I wouldn't enjoy coming all the way back to Mulberry in it. Everything will be fine. I promise," Elliot said.

Biting her lip, the pain didn't register as she mulled it over. "Okay. I don't want to see you get hurt either, Elliot, because of my silly worries."

"They aren't silly." He squeezed her hand again in reassurance. God, she needed that.

"Great decision. I'll get your discharge papers ready and be right back." Dr. Pearson left the room, but not before offering a ridiculous smirk.

Ignoring the smirk and the implications behind it, Lynn took the opportunity to borrow Elliot's phone and call her daughter. Lynn downplayed her injury to dispel the concern she heard in Laura's voice, making it more about the snow than anything else, which helped to reduce the alarm. Once Laura realized Lynn was going to be okay and she would be staying at Debbie's, her excitement increased.

Lynn also spoke to Debbie, who started to fret over her like a mother hen. She assured her that Laura would be fine and to be careful when she ventured back to Mason. She eased all of Lynn's worries that Laura would make it to school on time, or if school happened to close, then she would watch Laura herself. Lynn tried to argue the point, especially concerning Debbie's job, but Debbie refused to listen, telling her not to worry about a thing. Lynn tried not to.

Not once through the entire conversation had Debbie asked what sort of errands she had finished before getting in a wreck, or who Elliot was. Of course, she'd just hassle Lynn tomorrow face-to-face. And how would she describe Elliot to her? A new friend or something closer to the heart?

Thirty minutes later, they were leaving the hospital toward Elliot's home. Instead of sitting agitated and nervous in the passenger seat, she sat calmly and content. She barely knew him, but oddly enough, Elliot just had a way of making her feel safe, cared for, loved even. His kindness, his tenderness made her wish for things she normally wouldn't wish for. Talk about falling hard for a man if she truly let herself. But could she let herself?

When Trent died, Laura's father, the devastation had nearly destroyed her. The only other person whom she could share her concerns, fear, joy, and happiness had suddenly been ripped from her life. By a drunk driver, no less. Not a scratch on the man either, walking away with nothing but a hangover.

She had been twenty-one, no college education, a three-month-old baby, and no one else in the world who cared about her. Only Trent. Her parents had disowned her the minute she got pregnant with Laura and she told them Trent was the father. They had hated him from the start, a loser from the wrong side of town. They had been ashamed she let herself become pregnant with such a horrible man.

The thing she could never get them to understand, he wasn't a horrible man. He had been sweet, kind, and giving. They never married because Trent wanted to get her the nicest ring he possibly could. He had been saving money for the right ring. The worst part, something she could never think about without crying, he died driving home from the jewelry store.

She couldn't stand the sight of the town after that. Her parents, not once after he died, ever paid her a visit to offer sympathies or a shoulder of help. So, she had done what she thought best at the time.

She left.

She found Mason and a home for the first time. Wonderful people who accepted her for who she was. No judgment. No damaging words. Just pure friendliness and open arms.

As Elliot pulled into his driveway to a one-story rambling house, the dream she pictured to make those difficult lonely years bearable, emerged with vibrancy. A home with a loving man, a parcel of kids running around the yard carefree, a place to make memories until they both grew old together.

That dream swiftly morphed into this house with Elliot. He just made it easy to do, especially when he came to her side of the truck and gently scooped her into his arms with an ease that felt natural and like he'd done it a million times already.

"How are you feeling?" he asked as he walked to the porch with slow, careful steps.

Everything looked like it had been shoveled a while ago, but the snow falling as it had, filled up the pathway rather quickly.

"Still a bit dizzy, a bit nauseous. Not good, huh?" She sighed, pressing her head to his chest and inhaled his alluring aroma. A nice woodsy scent that reminded her of the park she brought Laura to all the time where she enjoyed running through the woods looking at all the animals and nature surrounding her. Laura loved being outdoors. She even brought a notebook to write down each animal she saw and identify it. She especially loved the birds.

"I'd feel better if those went away, but you'll be fine."

❄

ELLIOT BLEW OUT A SILENT BREATH. They weren't even in the hospital anymore and his nerves were wired high. She'd be fine. Just like he said. The alternative, well, he wouldn't think about that. Losing Lynn, oddly enough, would break his heart. He barely knew her, but the perfect way she fit in his arms made him yearn to get to know her better. That lock around his heart was almost chipped away and hanging on by a thread. Seeing her in the hospital had hammered it away quite easily.

It was about time he had a beautiful Christmas for once. No doubt, he'd get one with Lynn in attendance.

The door swung open before Elliot could turn the knob.

"Come on in. Get out of that crazy cold. How are you, darling? I'm Gregory, but you can call me dad," Gregory said with a jovial smile.

"Geez, Dad, really. Don't scare her," Elliot groaned as his cheeks flamed with heat, despite the cold outside. Thirty-five years old and his dad could still manage to embarrass him in front of a woman.

"Just trying to make her feel at home, that's all. When you called, I got the guest room ready. New sheets. Fluffed the pillows. A nice bucket in case, you know, you feel the urge to use it." Gregory winked, gaining a beautiful smile from her.

"I'm sorry to be intruding like this." She tried to keep her eyes open as she talked, but they fluttered more than Elliot liked.

"No trouble at all. You try to get some rest now." Gregory nodded at Elliot to get her settled.

Ten minutes later, Elliot joined his dad in the kitchen where he pounced on him right away. "Is she alright?"

"She's sleeping now. She almost threw up, but managed to settle her stomach. I'm worried, Dad." Elliot ran a hand over his face, then brushed it through his thick brown hair, making some of the strands stick straight up.

"It's just a minor concussion. You worry too much. That's your problem."

"It's snowing pretty badly out there. She wouldn't have been on the road if it weren't for me. I don't know why I thought I had to try and track her down tonight to make sure she made it home, but now I'm damn glad I did. If I hadn't..." His voice trailed off as worst-case scenarios pummeled him like a punch to the gut.

"Someone else would've found her in time. You worry me sometimes, Elliot. Lighten up for your old man once in a while. Maybe this was all meant to be."

Elliot rolled his eyes. "You don't fool me, Dad. You're playing matchmaker here, and it all started with that damn present. I don't even know why she donated it. I can clearly see she's tight on money, and yet she took the time to donate a gift."

"That's wonderful of her to think of others. I like her even more. I had nothing to do with that gift. I'm not matchmaking, but if I was, I'd say I was doing a damn good job." His dad chuckled as he started to walk out of the kitchen. "'Night, Elliot. Holler if you need me to help wake her up."

Elliot couldn't help but grin at his dad's words. He went to his room and set his alarm for two hours. He would've liked to sit in her room and watch over her, but he didn't want to make her feel smothered. She probably wanted her space.

Except, when he went into her room the first time to wake her up, she whispered delicately, "Lay with me for a while. I feel better when you're near."

So he did. At first, her head rested against his chest, but after noticing her discomfort, he moved her to the pillow. To still offer the comfort she needed, he grabbed her hand, gently holding her as she slept.

Every two hours his alarm went off. He would wake her up, ask how she was feeling, and after he felt satisfied, he would let her fall back to sleep. He had done this until the first sign of the sun told him morning had arrived. He waited another hour before waking her up.

He completed his normal routine of checking on her, whispered encouraging words that she was getting better and he'd be back in another two hours. She closed her eyes, mumbling something, but he couldn't make out the words. She needed her rest. Waking her up again to find out wasn't that important.

He strolled into the kitchen after freshening up with a

quick shower. His dad sat at the kitchen table by the sliding door where the white snow glistened in the morning sun.

"That's a lot of snow. More than three to four inches, I'd say." Elliot grabbed a cup from the cupboard and poured a steaming cup of coffee.

"Damn weatherman was wrong again. I think they said at least ten to twelve inches accumulated overnight. And it's still lightly snowing. How's our girl?"

"Our girl?"

"Oh, feeling possessive, are we? I noticed you didn't sleep in your room." His dad raised his brows with a smirk.

Elliot shook his head and took a sip of coffee before he blurted out something he'd regret. "Dad, stop, please. Don't say those things around her. You got me. I like her. So don't ruin my chances with your scheming. And yes, I slept in her room to wake her up every two hours. Nothing more."

Gregory chuckled, but didn't say another word.

An hour passed. Elliot and his dad were still enjoying their coffee at the table when Lynn walked into the kitchen.

Elliot stood up so fast he almost knocked his chair over. "Are you sure you should be walking without help?"

Lynn smiled. "I'm fine, Elliot. I actually feel a lot better. My head still hurts, but I imagine that's just from hitting it on the steering wheel so hard. I saw your phone in the bedroom. I used it to call Laura. I hope that's okay."

"You're welcome to use anything in the house. No need to ask. How is she?"

"Good. Happy. School was canceled. Debbie said she took the day off, and she even called Tara for me. I can't believe I forgot to call my own boss."

"Crazy night last night. Try not to worry. You want some coffee, darling?" Gregory asked, standing up from the table as well.

"Yes, thank you." Lynn smiled warmly.

Elliot frowned, unable to mask his concern as he moved closer to the counter, just on the other side of where she stood.

"It's still snowing, but I'm sure the roads are much better than last night. I can drive you home soon. I'd feel better if you stayed a while. It hasn't been a full twenty-four hours yet."

God, had that come out sounding desperate? Elliot rubbed a hand over his thigh, wiping the nerves away.

"Laura sounded happy. I'm okay staying here for a while. Maybe grab a shower. I noticed some blood on the bed sheets. I'm so sorry, Elliot."

He rounded the corner with quick steps and grabbed her hands. "They're just sheets. My dad's a whiz at getting stains out. Aren't you, Dad?"

"Best ever. Learned it all from your mother. Now, she could get permanent marker out of a shirt like there was nothing to it," his dad said with a chuckle.

"If you're sure. I can replace them—"

"I don't want new sheets. Take a shower, but be very careful. I don't want you to slip and fall."

She pulled one of her hands from within his grasp and cupped his cheek lightly. "You make me feel special every time I hear a hint of concern. I'll yell out if I have any trouble." Her face bloomed a deep red.

Elliot offered a tender smile. Was she imagining what that scene would look like if she hollered for help completely naked in the shower like he was? He wouldn't like it if she needed help, but he couldn't help wanting to help. "There are towels in the hallway closet. Take your time. I'll make you some breakfast. Think you can eat something?"

"I think so. Thank you, Elliot, for everything."

He leaned in closer so his dad couldn't hear. "You're worth it. You make me feel special every time I hear your beautiful voice." He kissed her cheek before stepping away.

※

Her legs were like jello as she walked out of the kitchen. Simple handholding had nothing over what a kiss from his lips had. Pure molten desire. Get her a freezer, stat!

Showering with care was difficult as the anticipation of spending as much time with Elliot before she went home had her rushing a tiny bit. When she almost slipped in the shower, she forced herself to slow down.

Fifteen minutes later, dressed in borrowed clothes that Elliot graciously gave her before she jumped in the shower, she walked back into the kitchen feeling like a whole new person. And still ridiculously hot. The snow shining outside looked like a wonderful escape to cool down.

Elliot pulled out a chair and set a plate of eggs and toast in front of her. "It's not much. Let my dad know if you want more and he can whip it up."

She frowned, glancing up into his tender blue eyes that still held so much worry. "Are you leaving?"

"Yeah, I have to run out for a short bit. I shouldn't be too long. My dad can always bring you home if you need to go right away, but I hope you'll wait for me." Elliot sighed, running a hand through his hair. "I just got a call. Fred's causing problems at the bar again."

"Is the bar even open this early?"

"Not yet. He's already drunk and demanding they open the doors so he can get even more drunk. I don't know what to do about him anymore."

"I know he's your friend, but you can't keep pulling him out of situations without the consequences. Maybe he needs to learn a lesson the hard way," his dad offered.

"Maybe. It's the holidays," Elliot said, grabbing his keys from the counter and shoved his phone onto his belt near his gun.

"Since when are you so jolly about the holidays?" his dad said, raising a brow with a quick glance at Lynn.

Lynn looked away, the heat filling her cheeks at what he insinuated. Did she really instill the Christmas spirit in Elliot?

Elliot followed his gaze, smiling gently at her. "What can I say? I feel the Christmas spirit suddenly."

Lynn smiled, yet produced a frown just as quickly as the sight of his gun slapped her in the face. "I hope there's no trouble. He wouldn't hurt you, right?"

"I don't expect any trouble." Elliot touched his gun. "Hazard of the job, having to carry this with me."

He walked over to her, ignoring the fact Gregory stood in the kitchen with them, and kissed her lightly on the lips. "I'll be back soon. Then I can take you home."

He left the kitchen as a small pit of worry formed in her stomach, weaving its way to her heart when the door closed with a loud click. Something bad was about to happen. Seeing that gun hanging at his side made it real. She willed the time to go faster and for him to walk back into the house harm free.

6

Lynn's hand shook as she tried to shove the key into the lock. Elliot stood behind her, very close, just in case she fell. She didn't think she would fall, especially with the snow piled on her doorstep as it was. Her feet were firmly planted in a pile of snow, holding her upright. The concern he displayed made those brief desiring tingles from his touch resurface without him even laying one finger on her. No one had fussed over her like this since Trent.

She finally managed to open the door, pushing hard. Stumbling inside, a strong pair of hands caught her before she fell—once again.

"Lynn, are you alright?"

The warmth from his hands turned up the heat as the cold from outside swirled around them. "Just a little clumsy, I guess. I don't know what's wrong with me."

"You have to take it easy. Why don't you get settled in and I'll shovel the sidewalk and driveway for you?" He kissed the top of her head, squeezing her lightly before stepping back. "Do you have a shovel in the garage?"

She turned toward him, closing the front door before the

cold wiped away his warm touch. "You've already done so much, Elliot. I can do it."

"That's not happening, Lynn. Please, just go rest and let me handle things. I don't mind."

His smile made her want to give in, but it was the concern that still lingered in his eyes that did it. "Okay. I suppose I should call a tow company to get my car since the snow finally stopped." Her voice dipped. More money she didn't have to spend on such a service, or to actually get it fixed. She hoped the problem wasn't too serious.

Elliot ran a hand through his hair, then shoved it into his coat pocket. "Uh, about your car. It's already been towed."

She gave him a look that made his fidgeting rather obvious. "Elliot, while I appreciate everything you've done so far, you can't keep doing this. It's my car. My responsibility."

"It's just—"

"I can take care of myself. I have for a very long time." Turning away from him, she stomped toward the kitchen to gather some patience. He really had been such a gentleman since she met him. Taking her anger out on him wouldn't show her appreciation, even though he deserved a bit right now.

Sure, no money existed to get her car towed, but she didn't want to be indebted to anyone, and that's exactly how she felt.

To curb the anger vibrating throughout, needing to keep busy before she stomped back out to him, she pulled open the fridge and stared at the contents. A small frown appeared as the emptiness stared back. Her spirits dipped further at the depressing picture stinging her eyes.

A soft voice tickled in her ear, lifting her briefly. "My dad called a tow company before I even woke up. Not that I wouldn't have done it myself because I would've. I'm not trying to take over your life and control it. But is it so wrong to accept help once in a while?"

She slowly turned around. The cold air from the fridge helped to cool her down from the heat that ignited in her body from his close proximity. It also cooled down her anger. Just a little.

"I have to pay you back."

He stepped closer, his body barely a breath away. "I don't want your money, Lynn."

Did he know what his nearness did to her? She swallowed as her eyes glossed to his lips.

No kissing.

But why?

Right. She was mad at him.

"I barely know you to accept such help."

"Easily fixed. You start to get to know me better." He brought a hand to her cheek, lightly caressing.

"I'm scared."

"Of what? Of me?"

Elliot's hand twitched as if he almost wanted to lower it, but must've changed his mind as he continued to hold it gently to her face. A faint thumping filled the silence in the kitchen. Was that his heart pounding or hers?

"Of having a relationship. It's been so long. I was terrified the entire morning you were gone. Seeing that gun, knowing what sort of situation you were walking into, it scared me. I lost Laura's father, and it broke me. I'm scared to get close to you and then lose you, too." A small breath escaped as she lowered her eyes to center on his chest. "You make me feel things I haven't felt in a long time."

He cradled her face, making her look at him. "I can't give you the security that nothing will happen because I don't know the future. I had to arrest Fred today. The damn man had to hit Stu, who pressed charges. We live in a small town, and I'm not too worried something horrible will happen. That doesn't mean I'm not on my toes when I respond to something."

He stroked his thumbs on her cheeks as a myriad of emotions crossed over his features.

"I'm scared, too, Lynn. I lost my mom three years ago to cancer. It's the hardest thing I ever went through. She didn't die around the holidays, but she always managed to make it a wonderful time of year. I can't stand Christmas anymore. Nobody would guess it because I hide it, except from you, apparently. For the first time, since she's been gone, you make me want a nice Christmas again. How about we try to sift through these feelings together?"

"I think I would like that." The words left her mouth breathlessly, her eyes locked with his.

"When you speak like that, and look at me the way you do, I lose my mind." He closed the distance, claiming her lips.

She leaned into him and grabbed the back of his shirt as their tongues tangled softly. He took his time exploring, tasting, mingling with her. A moan escaped as he moved his hands from her face, dragging them to her back and down her body where he pressed her into his hard body.

She met each stroke of his tongue, their movements increasing in desire as their hands explored each other just like their lips. She started to giggle into his mouth when the coldness hit her more prominently as he backed her into the wide-open fridge.

"I forgot to close the door," she said with a chuckle. She pushed him slightly away. His sweet smile weaved its way to her heart as she closed the door.

"I want to keep kissing you, but I think I'll go shovel the

snow now. If I start kissing you again, it'll definitely lead to the bedroom. That's not what I want yet. I don't want this, whatever's between us, to be about sex. I want it all, Lynn."

His eyes held hers intensely, conveying what he really meant by those words. It scared the hell out of her, yet delighted her beyond her wildest imagination.

"Slow is good. And just because you kissed me like that doesn't mean I forgot about our conversation. I'm still going to pay you back for my car."

❄

He snatched a quick kiss because he just couldn't help himself, nor had any good response to her comment. It'd be a cold day in hell before he let her pay him back for the car. All he wanted was to start something new, something great, and something a little exciting with her. Yet, all he seemed to be doing was arguing back and forth with her about money. He didn't want her money. Spoiling her sounded so much better. Life would be much easier if she would just let it go.

"The snow's calling my name." He grabbed another kiss, needing another small taste of her, and left the kitchen. Any other response would've created a new argument.

Forty minutes later, he came back inside to a fresh pot of coffee and the warmth of a gorgeous woman. He had shoveled the entire driveway and her sidewalk. His muscles ached from all the exertion. His snow blower would've come in real handy. Imagining Lynn shoveling the driveway herself almost made him break the shovel. Talk about another argument occurring if he inquired who shoveled the driveway all the time, or even a simple offer of doing it for her regularly. He knew the answer to everything. So damn independent. But what an amazing woman.

He promised to let her know the progress of the car when he knew more, arguing with her a few minutes about the issue, but standing firm in getting it fixed out of his pocket. "Call it a Christmas gift," was his argument the entire time. "I'm paying you back," was her annoyed response. He had kissed her to dispel the argument. That seemed to do the trick.

He then shifted the conversation. He still needed help in finding a gift to donate to the church. And the sooner he could see her, the better. She didn't have to know he just needed a good excuse to see her again so soon.

Yet, she gave him a sweet smile as if she knew what he was doing. She told him whenever he wanted to, to which he said, tomorrow.

As he drove away, he decided tomorrow couldn't come soon enough. Would she still want to see him? Who knew what his fate would be when she walked back into the kitchen. He just couldn't help himself. He had to do it covertly. Otherwise an argument surely would've started.

❄

LYNN'S SMILE never dissipated as he pulled out of her driveway. It died as soon as his truck disappeared. Suddenly, she missed him. He had brightened her day more than she experienced in a long time, small arguments included. Not that her daughter didn't make her happy, because she did. This was a different sort of happy. A desirable happy, that made her heart beat madly, her face flame with longing, and her body intensify in cravings. Tomorrow would take forever to come.

She walked back into the kitchen and grabbed her mug from the counter, refilling it with more caffeine that she probably didn't need. Taking a small sip, she picked up Elliot's empty mug and nearly dropped the hot coffee all over herself.

With a trembling hand, she set her mug down and swiped the twenty that had been hidden underneath his cup.

Damn him!

This was still too much of a tip for that simple coffee and pie he ordered yesterday. Why couldn't he let it rest? She didn't need or want this much money from him. A few dollars, like a normal customer, would be fine.

Half crumbling the twenty in her fingers, she released a slow breath. Elliot was just trying to be nice. That's it. Continuously going back and forth over this tip would get them nowhere, especially if she really wanted to start a relationship with him. And she did.

He won this small battle. A twenty she could accept with more ease than a fifty.

She shoved the twenty in her purse and called Debbie before her anger swept in and she called Elliot instead to cancel plans. Perhaps she would later. Keeping that money would be a difficult thing to do.

She updated Debbie on everything and almost cried with relief when she offered to drive Laura home. How had she found such a wonderful friend, or such a wonderful town? She knew without a doubt most people in this town would stop what they were doing and help her out if she needed it. Not that she would ever ask.

Laura came home, gushing over the huge gash and stitches adorning her forehead. She had already looked in the mirror several times, cringing each time at the horrible wound. She looked like a monster out of a horror movie. What in the world did Elliot see in her? Nasty gash, old clothes, worn shoes, no money. She sounded pathetic.

Then she almost slapped herself for thinking such thoughts. That's the only thing that was pathetic, thinking such depressing thoughts. He obviously saw something in her because he wouldn't keep coming around if he didn't. Or arguing about money, hiding money underneath a cup—mimicking her earlier actions when she had done it to him. That, of course, made her laugh. She should be mad at him for it, except all she could do was laugh.

She dismissed all crazy thoughts and decided to cheer herself up by baking.

She had already pulled out the flour and sugar when Laura came into the kitchen. "What are you making, Mom?"

"Sugar cookies. Do you wanna paint them with fun colors?"

A wide smile formed on Laura's face as she ran to grab an apron out of the drawer near the kitchen sink. She slapped on a red and white checkered print apron that Lynn had sewn last year for her. She loved baking just as much as she loved eating what they baked. Cookies never lasted long in their house, or any other delicious treat they created together.

"What's the occasion?" Laura asked as she started measuring the flour.

"I just thought cookies sounded good. Are you telling me you don't want any?" Lynn asked with a goofy grin, knowing quite well Laura would never say no to cookies.

Lynn pulled the vanilla extract from the cupboard to stop herself from squeezing her daughter tight. She had missed her. She rarely spent a day away from her.

"Of course, Mom," Laura drawled with a voice that sounded incredulous, like she would ever deny wanting cookies. "You've had a funny look on your face since I got home. A sort of glow or something."

Lynn paused in her steps, holding an egg she needed for the recipe. "A glow? I don't have a glow." She laughed as she joined Laura back in front of the counter.

"I don't know, Mom, there's a glow. I heard Aunt Debbie talking to you, asking about some guy named Elliot. Who's Elliot?"

Heat flamed Lynn's cheek. Talking about Elliot to Laura didn't seem like a wise step. What would she say? She rarely dated. Of course, she had been asked out before, but she normally declined. A few times she accepted, wondering the entire time she was out with them why she even had. They were dull, boring, and never measured up to Trent.

With no chance of stopping the impulse, she always compared every other man to Trent. She knew that wasn't right, but she missed him. She didn't think of him as much as she had in the beginning, but enough where he would always have a place in her heart.

Elliot's face suddenly flashed before her. Comparing him to Trent hadn't officially overwhelmed her yet.

Odd. It always happened right away.

Now, it was finally happening.

Voicing it out loud that he could almost surpass Trent pricked her heart as a betrayal. But she couldn't deny the truth. While Trent had treated her right, he hadn't always given her his full-attention. Elliot had, since the moment she met him, given her his full, undivided attention. His concern for her as well, so endearing that she couldn't help but smile anytime she thought about it. Trent never displayed that level of concern. They were also young teenagers in love. Now she was like an old woman with too much experience behind her back.

"Mom, earth to Mom. What are you smiling about? Who's Elliot?" Laura asked, waving a hand in her face.

Lynn ruffled Laura's hair with a silly smile. "He's the one who found me in my car."

"Oooh, you like this Elliot dude. Don't you?" Laura crooned.

The heat rushed down her body as she turned away from Laura. In the limelight with her own daughter. What did she say to her? Of course, she liked Elliot. A lot! But would it be good to let a man enter their lives? Laura never, not once, met any man she dated.

"Maybe a little." Whew! Crisis averted. That should be enough to pacify her and keep her out of the danger zone of dating talk.

"Mom has a boyfriend. Mom has a boyfriend. That's so cool!" Laura jumped up with excitement, knocking the flour bag over, spilling the contents onto the counter.

"Laura, be careful, please," Lynn said as she gently picked up the flour bag and started to scoop the spilled flour back into the bag. "And he's not my boyfriend. I said maybe I liked him a little."

"Mom, you have a glow. You got bright red in the face when I said his name and a goofy smile. You totally zoned out on me." Laura rolled her eyes. "Seriously, Mom, it's about time you went out on a date. I'm a big girl. I can handle it."

Lynn wiped her hands on her apron, at a loss for words. When had her seven-year-old gotten so big, so mature? "You can, can you? I don't need to date. I don't need a man. I have you. You make me the happiest."

"I know, Mom. But you deserve a little more happiness. You work too much. And are these cookies for him?" Laura asked playfully.

"No, of course not." Lynn turned around, cracking the egg open. "It's Christmas time. We always make cookies."

"Did he ask you out?"

"Laura, really, when did you get so mature on me? You're seven, not eighteen."

"Mom, even I have a boyfriend."

"What! Since when? And who?" Lynn asked, turning to her with surprise.

"Tim, in my class. He's always giving me some of his fruit snacks at lunch," Laura said with a small blush forming on her face this time.

"Well, no kissing. You're too young to have a boyfriend. Oh, geez, stop growing up on me. I can't handle this stuff," Lynn said as she grabbed Laura by the shoulders and pulled her into a hug. "Just stay my little girl forever, okay?"

Laura laughed as she started to measure the sugar. "So, did he ask you out?"

"Ugh! Yes, he did. Sort of. He needs my help picking out a gift to donate to the church. I really wouldn't call that a date." Geez! Her own seven-year-old daughter was strong-arming her into spilling her guts on Elliot.

"You need to date more often, Mom. He's so making an excuse to hang out with you."

"Oh, really, since when are you a love expert?" Lynn laughed, nudging Laura playfully on the shoulder.

"Uh, since I have a boyfriend and you don't."

"You got me there." Lynn laughed harder, loving her daughter even more. Maybe letting Elliot into their lives wouldn't be as hard as she originally thought. The idea sounded more appealing as the conversation went on.

"When are you shopping with him?"

Lynn looked at her daughter, the light shining brightly in her eyes. Laura was truly excited for her. Did that mean she displayed she wasn't happy around her? She hadn't thought so.

"He suggested tomorrow. Obviously, after my shift and you get home from school. Would you like to help pick out a gift?"

"Yeah, totally. Can we go to Wacky Wowza's? I bet we can find something super awesome there."

The excitement in Laura's voice had Lynn shaking her head yes. Wacky Wowza's, a silly, creative shop that surprisingly did well in their little town. They sold anything and everything you could think of: prank gifts, clothes, food, books, toys, and even one aisle held sexual toys. Lynn had actually braved that aisle one time just to see what it entailed, but after about five seconds of looking around, her nerves took over from the ludicrous notion of standing there. What happened if someone saw her?

The heat swirled around her body, igniting her desire.

The sex toy aisle.

Oh, boy, she could just imagine walking down that aisle with Elliot.

Building her own large walk-in freezer would come in handy with all this need to cool herself down continuously. How long would Elliot keep heating her up like this?

Forever sounded like a good possibility.

With vigorous strokes, she stirred the mixture. Doing it fast should hide the shivers wracking her body.

Because forever sounded just nice.

7

"This is so cool, Mom. Watch it talk," Laura exclaimed as she talked to the monkey on the shelf and laughed hysterically as it talked back.

"Pretty neat, I agree," Lynn said with a smile.

Elliot leaned into her. Holding it in wasn't possible anymore. "You haven't said anything about the money yet. I actually expected you to cancel on me today."

"It crossed my mind, Elliot. I don't want to argue about that blasted tip any more. Twenty was still way too much." She sighed heavily as her eyes glazed with happiness. "Look how happy she is. It's really hard to be mad at you when that twenty you gave me helped me buy that exact monkey."

She nudged him in the stomach with a playful smile. "I'm paying you back for my car, though. We're not even arguing about that."

"I hate arguing with you. That's why I'll just pay for it." He smiled back as he wrapped an arm around her. Perhaps teasing wasn't wise, but he would win that battle. She just didn't know it.

"Have you ever been here, Elliot? Look at all the cool

stuff. Did you see the toy aisle? Did you want to donate a toy? Or maybe a nice sweater? What about those cans of peanuts? I'm sure some people need food for Christmas," Laura rattled off in one breath.

Elliot laughed. Her excitement was infectious. Amazing that Lynn hadn't canceled on him for hiding the money and that she felt comfortable enough to bring Laura along. He knew how some parents, single parents, could be very protective of their children. He fell under Laura's spell just as quickly as he had for her mother. They were both perfect. Best Christmas present he could've asked for. Not that he had asked for a present this year.

"I've never been here. I don't venture to Mason often, but this is a very interesting store. Love the monkey." There went another clink to the lock on his heart as her eyes lit up at his words.

"But you'll come more often now that you're dating my mom, right? She needs a man," Laura said, placing a hand on her hip with a sassy look that said she knew everything.

"Laura! I don't need a man. Don't embarrass Elliot. Or me, for that matter," Lynn said, blushing a bit at her daughter's outspokenness.

Elliot wrapped his arm tighter around Lynn. Her softness, the delicacy of holding such a beautiful, sweet woman, wove its way straight to his soul. "If your mom lets me, I definitely plan on more visits. Is that okay?"

"Yeah, I like seeing my mom happy. Oh, wow, what's that?" Laura said, rushing over to another area in the same aisle.

"Sorry about that. I've never really let her meet anyone I've dated before," Lynn said, walking down the aisle slowly with Elliot as Laura continued bouncing from one thing to another with excitement. "You shouldn't have come into the diner today and left another big tip. And I'm paying for my car, Elliot."

"We agreed not to argue about the car." He placed a finger over her lips when she started to open her mouth. "I can't help myself. I just have the urge to spoil you. I don't think that's going to change. And I only left a small tip today."

Elliot frowned as the anger still simmered in her beautiful brown eyes. He seriously couldn't control the urge to spoil her. Making her mad was the last thing he wanted to do, especially this early in the dating game, but he just couldn't help it. He liked spoiling and taking care of her.

He dropped his hand from her lips and prepared his heart to be booted out of the store.

"I've been alone a long time, Elliot. It feels like charity. And you left five dollars for a coffee that barely cost two dollars."

He grabbed her cheeks in a gentle manner. "I just enjoy spoiling you. I would never insult you like that. Trust me when I say I wanted to leave more than five dollars."

He lightly kissed her to stop any more angering words. A light touch normally did the trick. So very evil of him, but he refused to hear or see any more anger from her. The tension between them held firmly for about a second until she gave in, leaning into him with a sweet sigh. He started to slide his tongue in to capture a more delightful kiss and erase all of the discord between them when a giggle erupted.

He pulled away from Lynn. Laura stood there with a box of candy and a smile that spoke volumes.

"Mom said I can't kiss. How come you two can?"

"Uh...well...uh..."

Lynn laughed at Elliot's discomfort. "Because we're

adults and you're not. You shouldn't even have a boyfriend at seven."

"What do you think, Elliot? I should be able to have a boyfriend, shouldn't I?"

Elliot ran a hand through his hair as the panic swelled to epic proportions. How did Lynn do this parent thing? "That's a hard question. Does he treat you nice?"

"Yep. Tim shares his fruit snacks. One time he even picked up my notebook that fell on the floor." Laura looked away as her face said she was reminiscing those wonderful times.

"Does he respect you?" Elliot glanced at Lynn, who had a mischievous smirk on her face. God, she wanted to see how he would end this. Would this be a pass or fail kind of thing? Retribution for leaving nice tips?

"Yeppers. He doesn't call me dumb like Stewart does. He's the dumb one."

Lynn tensed next to him. He placed a hand onto her back. "Why does Stewart call you dumb?" Maybe he should've let Lynn take over like it appeared she wanted to.

"I don't know. I always get the answers right when the teacher calls on me. He always gets mean when Tim's around me." Laura shrugged, her smile dimming a little.

Elliot cracked a small smile. "Your mother is going to have a difficult time warding off all the boys as you get older. Sounds like Stewart is jealous of Tim. Does Tim act like a gentleman even when Stewart is around?"

Laura's face brightened at those words. "He's always nice to me. He even defends me when Stewart's mean. You think Stewart likes me?"

"You're wonderful, Laura. I'm sure he does. I would stick with a boy that treats you nice, respects you, and doesn't call you mean names, though. Stewart sounds like he needs to learn some pointers from Tim."

"So, you're saying it's okay to have a boyfriend?" Laura smiled brightly, giving her mom a look that said, "See, it's okay."

"Uh, well, I guess. But Tim does need to keep his hands to himself. No touching or kissing." Elliot couldn't risk a glance at Lynn. Had he overstepped his boundaries? She still hadn't said a word, and while she continued to let him hold her, he couldn't sense her mood.

"But why?" Laura asked, truly confused.

Elliot dropped his arm from around Lynn and got down on his knee, getting eye level with Laura. "Because being respectful and treating you nice is the first step in any relationship. He needs to display those qualities until he can earn anything else. Do you want to kiss him?"

"Not really. It looks sort of gross. Why do you kiss my mom?"

Elliot's feet started to itch as his face burned with embarrassment. This little girl was just as bold as her mother with her words. He couldn't help but respect that, yet the answer teetered on his lips.

"Because she's beautiful, smart, funny, and an amazing woman. I guess it's my way of saying all of that in a nice simple kiss. Just like Tim, I need to show respect and be nice. If she doesn't think I'm doing a good job, it's her right to kick me to the curb."

"I'll never ever let a boy treat me mean. Can we get this candy for part of the present?" Laura asked, holding up the box of candy with assorted chocolates.

Elliot laughed and stood up. "I think that candy is a great start to the gift. Let's see what else we can find."

"I saw this awesome blanket at the end of the aisle." Laura rushed back down the aisle.

"Lynn, I'm sorry if—"

She grabbed his face, planting a quick kiss on his lips. "You handled that perfectly. You have a way with kids, Elliot."

"Really? I thought I was screwing that up royally. I'm glad you're not mad. Boys, already? I'd be going out of my mind. I am, actually, for you. I feel like doing a background check on this Tim boy just to make sure he's decent." Elliot rubbed a hand over his face, then gave her a smile as she continued to look at him like he was her savior.

"Come on. Let's keep you earning your way to more than a kiss." Lynn looped her arm through his as they followed Laura around the store. His smile grew wider at that comment.

He didn't think he was anywhere near earning his way towards more than a kiss, but if Lynn thought so, he'd roll with it. And when they came across the sex toy aisle, his pants became instantly uncomfortable. Oh yeah, he wanted to earn a lot more than just a kiss as soon as possible.

He cleared his throat as he shifted awkwardly on his feet. "Are you kidding me? This store truly holds it all, doesn't it?"

"Is that a blush I see?" Lynn laughed.

"Men do not blush. Therefore, I am not blushing. Would you care to take a stroll down this aisle? I'm suddenly feeling hungry. Do you think they carry edible underwear?"

Lynn slapped his shoulder playfully. "Elliot Duncan, don't speak so loudly. Saying such things. What happens if Laura heard you? I would love to watch you talk your way out of that one."

His smile dipped. What a horrible conversation that

would be if it ever occurred. He slowly replaced his smile with a devious grin as he leaned in and whispered delicately in her ear, "I see a future shopping trip, just the two of us. This might be my new favorite aisle in the store. You've been down this aisle before, haven't you? What was your favorite thing, Lynn? I'm dying to know."

He kissed her neck before backing away. She looked into his eyes as she leaned into him this time. "I think my favorite thing was the glow-in-the-dark condoms. I was really curious how they would look in the dark. What do you think it would look like? Or maybe the pair of pink fluffy handcuffs. Would you like to handcuff me, Elliot?"

She backed up a step. His jaw dropped that she would say something so bold, so brazen.

"Men do blush, Elliot, or at least, you do. It's very cute."

❄

Elliot walked into the living room and took a seat on the couch near his dad. The Christmas movie playing, grabbing his dad's undivided attention, made him smile. His mother loved watching crazy 'B' flick movies all the time. His dad would grumble having to watch them with her, and now, here he was watching one without her.

Just another reason why love was difficult. Complicated. Worth every moment.

Lynn seemed to be pushing her way inside his heart, making him yearn for moments like this. Where he could sit down, pop in a cheesy Christmas movie, and enjoy the night snuggling together. Just the way his parents used to do.

The pain his dad must feel watching this movie. The memories that probably surfaced.

A quick glance revealed nothing but a smile on his dad's face.

Maybe not that painful. Maybe letting love in was worth it.

He loved his dad relentlessly. Worrying. Fussing. Prodding. Something he should do now. He still hadn't inquired about his memory issues.

"I can't take the suspense. How was your night?" his dad asked, offering some popcorn that he had left in his bowl.

Elliot declined with a simple shake, leaning further into the couch as he unclenched his hands. "We had a nice night."

Gregory raised a brow and put the bowl back on his lap. "Please, leave all the juicy details out. This old geezer doesn't need to live vicariously through you."

Elliot chuckled. "I would think you live vicariously through the other old geezers still working at the fire station."

Gregory laughed and winked, grabbing a handful of popcorn.

"Did you call Ernie back? He called earlier."

"Yep. Some details would be nice."

Elliot chuckled. "She brought her daughter with. She's just as sweet and special, like Lynn." He shifted on the couch, daring a peek at his dad. "Did you reschedule your dentist appointment yet?"

"Sure did."

"Oh, and Maurice called from the—"

"Just what are you trying to get at with all these questions, Elliot? You've never been very good at hiding things with me."

He cleared his throat to suppress a groan and looked at

his dad. "Sometimes you forget things and it has me a little worried."

"Stop worrying so much, Elliot. It's not good for you. And here, I thought with Lynn in the picture, you would mellow out a bit."

"She's amazing. I suppose I should say thanks for messing with me."

"I had nothing to do with that present."

"I can't believe you're still maintaining innocence in that."

"Did you invite her over for Christmas?"

"Ignoring it, doesn't make it go away."

Gregory cocked a brow. "What are we talking about now? The memory issue or the present? You've been jumping conversations like a frog on a mission."

"Both. And who's the one jumping conversations here?"

"So, when do I get to meet my new granddaughter? Invite them over for Christmas."

Elliot sighed as he ran a hand through his hair. Just once, he wanted his dad to take his health seriously. This conversation reminded him about the time they argued about him moving in.

"Dad, please, can you not talk like that, especially in front of them. I don't need you saying things like that scaring them away. I really like Lynn. And I'm going to monitor your health, whether you like it or not."

"I guess that's what kids are for. To annoy you." Gregory laughed. "Lynn's the one. I also bought my sweet granddaughter a new bike. You did mention how the one sitting in the garage looked small. It's pink and purple with little ribbons on the end and a cute little bell. Oh, and I bought a basket to attach to the front, so she can carry her notebook and stuff when they go to the park."

"Geez, you know how to annoy right back. Let me make sure it's okay with Lynn."

Gregory's eyes twinkled with mischief. "What's wrong with getting her a bike?"

"I'm on thin ice with her, Dad. Maybe it doesn't seem like it, but I am. She's a little touchy when it comes to money and receiving…things. I don't want to upset her. Please, tone it down some."

"I have to see this part. Quiet now."

That sounded like his dad wasn't going to listen to a word he said. Something he enjoyed doing since he sat down on the couch. But he'd be damned if things were screwed up even further with Lynn because of more money and gift issues.

Being annoyed at his dad would be easy, but each time he said something, like, calling Laura his granddaughter, it sounded good to his ears. These crazy emotions swirling around inside were flying too fast.

Could love happen this fast? Because the way his heart beat erratically just picturing Lynn's gorgeous face made him think, yes, love could happen this fast. He missed them both like hell.

His dad was trying to inject his wily ways and could potentially screw things up.

"Dad, seriously, you have to tone it down. I'm talking to Lynn about the bike. If she says no, you have to take it back."

"Sure, sure. I also bought a bunch of other stuff as well, not just a bike. They're all wrapped and tucked away in my closet for Christmas day. So make sure you invite them over for Christmas."

"Dad…"

Gregory glanced at him with a tender smile. "I would never ruin what you have with her."

"Then tone it down."

Now he just had to make sure he didn't ruin it himself. He'd ask Lynn tomorrow about Christmas. Surprisingly, the thought of Christmas looming didn't bring an ounce of panic or sadness. She was bringing the holiday spirit back into his life.

The lock around his heart splintered into pieces as the perfect gift for her came to him.

8

Lynn brushed a hand across her forehead. Her bangs lifted briefly, then settled across her eyes where they normally resided.

Damn! She ruined her bangs.

It took her over thirty minutes in the bathroom to get them to look just perfect and she swipes them flat in one second. Nerves were the culprit. She could only blame it on that. She didn't know where she got the ridiculous idea to bake more cookies and bring them to Elliot.

For the past two days, Elliot had visited her and Laura in Mason, spending the entire evening, about an hour longer after Laura went to bed. She made dinner for them the first night, a light chicken dinner, considering she didn't have much more in the house to offer. The embarrassment couldn't get any worse.

Then, last night, Elliot picked up pizza on his way, spoiling them again. The embarrassment went up a notch. Did he know she couldn't afford more fancy food than what she offered? Her anger almost unleashed until Laura's bright smile flashed before her when she saw the pizza boxes. Pizza was a treat for them.

The last two days had been a joy. Not just for Lynn, but Laura as well. She laughed at everything Elliot said, talked his ear off about school, and barely coerced him into playing games. Through it all, Elliot laughed back with her, listened intently when she spoke, and dove into each game with enthusiasm. He interacted with her daughter so beautifully. It almost seemed too good to be true.

True to his word, like he had spoken to Laura about boys treating girls, he only kissed her goodnight, never trying for anything else. Lynn decided he had earned his way to more. Probably since the moment she met him, if she was being honest. He just had a way of looking at her and spiking her body to a heated desire without effort.

Last night, before he left, he whispered regrettably in her ear that he had to work in the morning. He wanted to spend the entire day with her, but would settle for the evening if she and Laura were available. Lynn had smiled and assured him that was fine. Reassurance had seemed necessary. For him and a little for herself. His eyes had shimmered with an underlying sadness as if he thought he was dominating their time too much. She supposed for having just met him, maybe he had been. Despite their small arguments about money, she looked forward to when his truck pulled into the driveway. So did Laura.

This morning, after she dropped Laura off at her friend Ashley's house for a sleepover, she started to pull ingredients out for cookies. The compulsion to make Elliot cookies and deliver them to his work had taken over before she could stop herself. Over the course of the few days, they had talked about anything and everything. She had never opened herself up to another man like she had with Elliot. If she wasn't mistaken, he had never opened himself up to another woman as he had with her.

As she had started to whip the batter with vigorous strokes, one thought wouldn't go away. He had spoken so dynamically about his mother and how she would deliver treats to the police station. Making cookies had felt right.

More than once, he had commented about the way her eyes would light up when she talked about Christmas. His kind words always managed to evoke so many emotions from her. She wanted to help bring back the Christmas spirit he once loved because that sad look in his eyes was almost unbearable at times. Everybody should love Christmas, especially Elliot, a kind-hearted man who couldn't help but spoil her and Laura rotten.

That part really had to stop. He still refused to take any money for the car, which resulted in a few arguments that left her worried he wouldn't come back the next day. But it was simply too much. She couldn't let him pay for it.

Just like she almost couldn't let his father buy Laura so many gifts. Of course, the way Elliot portrayed it, his eyes sparkling with happiness, she found herself saying it was okay. That was part of the Christmas spirit. Wasn't it? How could she honestly take that away from him? Laura's bike really needed an upgrade. It seemed she grew an inch every day.

How empty and sad their lives would be if Elliot decided to walk away.

Stop!

He wasn't walking away. If anything, he was ramming his way into their lives, refusing to take no for an answer.

That's where the cookies came in. Doing something nice

for him for once. Perhaps make up for the arguments about her car. And that's all they were—arguments. She didn't have any money to pay him back yet. She still had to find money somewhere to buy Laura two more Christmas presents.

The stress just kept climbing each day.

She got her car back yesterday, surprisingly operating better than before her accident. So better, she had a strong feeling Elliot had more than just the accident issues fixed. She gained a flat tire and a few other issues under the hood from the accident that went over her head when Elliot relayed the information.

When she asked what the total bill came to, he simply refused to tell her. The man wouldn't budge even after she almost walked him to the door. Then he turned his sweet smile up a notch and grabbed a kiss. Just like that, her worries floated away.

Until she saw the car sitting in her driveway. He had derailed the argument with a kiss. That meant it cost a lot to fix. At least a couple hundred.

A small brown box hidden in the corner of her closet kept her up late last night. Barely a wink of sleep. What was locked tightly inside burned a hole in her gut. She had one way to get some money to pay Elliot back and buy Laura's presents. One terrifying way that she didn't know if she could actually go through with it.

Best not to think about it right now. She had cookies to deliver.

Her steps staggered from the car to the doors of the police station. Wiping a clammy hand on her jeans, her bangs slightly lifted again as another breath escaped. Would he be mad that she was showing up out of the blue? Or would he be excited? Maybe he took this shift to make an excuse not to hang out with her on a Saturday. Since when did the chief of police work on a Saturday? He was the boss. He shouldn't have to work if he didn't want to. Maybe his shift would run into the evening and he'd have to cancel plans with her.

Standing frozen in front of the door, she couldn't make her hand reach for the handle. Did he not want to spend time with them anymore? Was that why he had to work on a Saturday?

The container of cookies started to get heavy, the outcome of her decision weighing on her. If she walked through the doors, possible rejection stood in her face. If she walked back to her car, possible rejection later that evening stood in her face. Rejection either way.

She turned around. Possible rejection later sounded much better. Delay the inevitable. Pretend everything was okay.

Her rust-bucket of a car glared in the shining sun. What was she thinking? He took the time to have her car towed and fixed. He paid for everything, every last dime to make it easier on her. He refused to tell her the total so she could pay him back. Argued relentlessly with her about it. How could she, for one minute, think that he would reject her? He had even asked them to join him for Christmas day at his house. That wasn't someone who didn't want to see her. That was someone who enjoyed her in his life.

This dating business was too much. Added stress she certainly didn't need.

She turned back around and grabbed the door handle firmly. No turning back now. She pulled the door open, wiped her feet on the carpet, and bee-lined it to the front desk before she twirled around to the exit with one smooth twist.

"Good morning. Or maybe I should say good afternoon. How may I help you?" the petite blonde woman behind the counter asked.

The words froze on the tip of her tongue. This woman worked with Elliot daily? Blonde hair, although swept into a delicate ponytail, looked lovelier than Lynn's ratty hair, especially with her bangs flat now. Her green eyes sparkled with friendliness, and a wide smile that said to Lynn men loved to kiss. She could just imagine what the rest of the woman's body looked like if she stood up. She couldn't compete with this woman.

Wait? That was crazy. Elliot didn't want to date this woman. Did he? Maybe he did, and couldn't because she worked with him. What a terrible idea to come!

"Are you alright, ma'am? How can I help you?" the nice woman said, finally standing up a little.

Lynn's face flamed with heat as her eyes trailed from the top of the woman's face and down the rest of her body. She was bound to reopen her gash on her forehead from fainting with disgust. She had the body of a model. Thin, voluptuous, and if she could see underneath the pants she wore, she figured legs to die for. Definitely, a terrible idea.

The woman started to reach for the phone, to call the mental ward probably, snapping her out of her stupor. "I'm here to see Elliot. Is...is he in?"

The woman stopped reaching for the phone as a small smile emerged. "He is. Can I have your name to let him know you're here?"

"Um...it's Lynn. I'm—"

"Oh, Lynn, his girlfriend. I didn't think I'd get to meet you so soon. He's mentioned you a time or two, not like his dad. His dad just loves talking about you. His dad and my dad volunteer together at the church. My dad relays a lot of what his dad says, so it's sort of second hand words. But they were all good words, of course. The chief is more shy, or not necessarily shy, just doesn't talk about his personal life as much. But any time he speaks about you, his face just lights up. It's nice to see. I never see him get excited like that. I am just talking too much. I could go on and on and on. I'm Daphne, it's so nice to meet you," she said as she held her hand out.

Lynn smiled, a real smile, as she shifted the cookies in her arm and shook Daphne's hand. The trembles in her hand had to be obvious. How pathetic did that make her?

Girlfriend. She had no idea Elliot thought of her like that. It sounded quite nice.

"It's nice to meet you, too, Daphne. I'm sorry for zoning out there. I was just appreciating your necklace. It's gorgeous." Such a dumb excuse for her weirdness earlier, but anything to explain her staring that was borderline rude. And it wasn't a lie. It was a very gorgeous necklace. Long gold chain, with five tiny diamonds lining down in a single line. It looked expensive.

Daphne placed a hand over her necklace. "Thank you. My boyfriend gave it to me for my birthday. What do you have there in your arms?"

Lynn glanced at the container. "Cookies. I thought Elliot might enjoy them."

"Oh, boy, a woman after his own heart. He'll love 'em. You can go on back. He'll be delighted to see you."

"Are you sure? I don't want to intrude if he's busy."

"Nonsense. He won't mind. Just follow that hallway to the end and take a right. His door is the last one on the left." Daphne pointed to the right with a bright smile.

Lynn nodded in thanks, her footsteps echoing down the hallway as freedom slowly ebbed away.

Nonsense! He would be happy to see her.

What an idiot! Such silly, ridiculous thoughts about that woman. Daphne had a boyfriend. Elliot wanted her, not any other woman. Talk about insecurity. She had no need to feel that way. But maybe she did because it had been so long since she left her heart open to a man. What would happen when she lost him? The outcome scared her.

She turned the corner, slowing her steps as she neared the last door on the left. Heart pounding like a jackhammer, she raised her hand to knock, except his door stood wide open. He sat at his desk, a hand shoved in his hair, staring at something. He had a frown plastered on his face and deep wrinkles lining his forehead. She wanted to wrap him up in her arms and take the sadness away. That sadness in him always made her heart ache.

A few taps on the doorframe did the trick to get his attention when he didn't notice her standing there. "Knock, knock. I hope I'm not intruding."

Elliot stood up so fast with an instant smile replacing his frown. "Definitely not. Just the sort of surprise I needed." He rounded the desk and pulled her into his arms for a deep kiss.

No hesitation. No rejection.

He took his time saying hello. Something she seriously enjoyed as the warmth of his body filled up her aching heart.

"Well, I certainly like this greeting." She backed up a step, only because she didn't want to drop the container of cookies. Staying in his arms forever sounded like a great plan.

"And I certainly like this visit. What's that?" He eyed the container, anticipation in his eyes.

"Cookies. I had an urge to bake and thought of you. I really hope I'm not intruding."

❄

"You can never intrude on me, Lynn."

He grabbed the container, lifted the lid and inhaled the wonderful scent. He pulled one out. The sweet flavors swirled inside his mouth, trailing down to his heart. A container full of cookies. His smile couldn't possibly get any wider. She made these for him. And definitely made just by her with no help from Laura. The delicate colors on each cookie looked meticulous. Not like the ones he had the other day she had made with Laura. Those cookies hadn't been painted with such precision. Was he dreaming? The perfect woman for him, and found so easily. He should've stopped for coffee at that diner ages ago.

"I guess I can let you get back to work."

Elliot grabbed her arm before she could walk away, lightly tossing the container onto his desk. Wrapping her close, he inhaled the wonderful cookie scent that lingered on her. "What's the rush? I need a break. Did you eat lunch yet?"

Geez, why hadn't his nerves gone away yet when she was near? What a dumb question. It was already two o'clock in the afternoon. Of course she probably ate.

"You didn't eat yet? That's not healthy for you, Elliot." She swiped a lock of hair back that fell onto his forehead. "I had a small lunch, but I'll keep you company. You should eat."

"I definitely need the company." He smiled, kissing her lightly on the lips. "Where's Laura?"

A light blush graced her cheeks. "She's spending the night with a friend. I have the night to myself."

"Really?" He smoothed a hand down her back, stretching his fingers like a web. She felt so delicious molded into his body. If the door wasn't wide open, he would've pulled her even closer. "Any specific plans you had?"

"Well, what sort of plans do you have?"

"Anything that has to deal with you." He kissed her again before reluctantly letting her go.

Tossing his papers in a haphazard pile, his heart thumped like a teenager eager for their first date. "I'm going to call it a day. I didn't even want to come in today, but I had to. When I started as the chief of police I wanted to be out in the streets. I work one Saturday every month with a different officer patrolling. I enjoy it and I think they do, too."

"Why Saturdays?"

"Why not? They work on weekends. I thought it would only be fair. Not much happens around here, though, so it's sort of just getting to know my officers on a one-to-one basis more than anything. Today, I got up rather early, around three, and rode with two different guys. I just got back to the office about an hour ago. Now that you're here, I'm ready to take the rest of the day off."

"You have to be tired, Elliot. If you want to go home and crash, that's fine."

"Do you want to know why I got up so early? It's because I couldn't sleep without thinking about you. Now that you're here, and have the entire night free, I'm not passing up this opportunity. So, Laura is having a sleepover?" He rounded his desk as his lips curled into a delicious grin.

"Yes, she is."

"Does that mean you can have a sleepover? Or maybe that's—"

She put a finger to his lips. "I would love to spend the night. You've earned it, and much more."

"I don't know what I did to deserve someone like you."

Pulling her back into his arms, he stole a kiss. His tongue slid in with ease, deepening the kiss to a higher level. Just a small taste of what was in store for tonight. Kissing her was like a drug he couldn't get enough of. The day got better the moment she walked through his door. A sleepover. Hell, yeah, he loved sleepovers.

Nipping her bottom lip, savoring her sweet taste one more time, he pulled away before the door magically shut and he showed her just what kind of sleepover would occur tonight. "Let's grab a bite to eat, then head home."

"I like that plan."

He grabbed his jacket hanging on the coat rack in the corner, shoved it on and swiped his cookies from his desk. "I plan to eat all of these later. You're more than welcome to surprise me with cookies anytime."

"I enjoy baking, so you might be in luck."

His heart swelled with joy. Future visits from her would be like visiting heaven every day. He wrapped his arm around her as they walked to the front.

"Daphne, you have a great night. I'm heading out for the day," Elliot said, trying not to grin like an idiot at Daphne, who clearly saw his silly grin anyway.

"You have a wonderful night, Chief. So good to meet your girlfriend. Just a sweetheart. Hope to see you again, Lynn." Daphne waved to them as they walked out.

"Sorry about that." The sidewalk opened to swallow him whole. Clearly, it wouldn't be just his dad out to embarrass him.

"About what? She's very nice. I zoned out in front of her and she was pleasant the entire time."

"About the girlfriend bit. Did that bother you?" He stopped walking and grabbed her hand. Maybe a bit too tightly. Could she feel the nerves running through him?

"No, actually, it sounded quite nice. Did it bother you?"

"Not in the least. I'm just sorry that people keep doing that to you. You know, my dad telling you to call him dad. I would never rush you into anything."

"Don't worry, Elliot."

Elliot started to lean in for a kiss when the last person he ever wanted to see walked up to them.

"Elliot, how are you? I missed you these last few days. Just where in the world have you been?" Marybeth asked, her eyes barely spared Lynn a glance. Dressed in a deep red coat, just like the other day, left a man to his imagination of what could be underneath.

Elliot pulled Lynn closer, squeezing her hand in reassurance. Not that she needed it because she blew Marybeth out of the park with looks, grace, and elegance. Maybe it was more for his benefit. How would Lynn take Marybeth's words? She made it sound like there was something going on between them when there wasn't.

"Hello, Marybeth. I'd like you to meet my girlfriend Lynn." He glanced at Lynn. "This is Marybeth. She's been a friend of the family for a long time. Her father and my father golf all the time in the summer."

He turned back toward Marybeth, his smile never wavering. The slight anger couldn't be mistaken in Marybeth's eyes. Did she finally understand he didn't want to date her?

"I had no idea you were seeing anyone, Elliot."

"I am." Simply put. She couldn't misinterpret that.

Marybeth looked at her watch, exclaiming with overdone enthusiasm. "Oh, my, look at the time. I need to get going. Nice to meet you, Lynn."

"You, too, Marybeth," Lynn replied softly.

"Will I see you at the Christmas party tonight, Elliot? You didn't forget, I hope." Marybeth smiled brightly at him.

"I hate to admit, I might have. Lynn and I will try to make it." Elliot smiled back as his arm tightened around Lynn.

Marybeth moved her eyes slowly from Elliot to Lynn. Her hazel eyes lacked their usual spark, but her smile never wavered. "That'd be great. I hope you can make it. I must run now. See you tonight, Elliot."

Marybeth started to glide by him, but not without running a hand down his arm as she passed by. Her intent was clear. She still didn't get the message he had no feelings for her. Even though Lynn stood in his arms, the other side of him suddenly felt dirty where Marybeth had touched him. A shower seemed necessary.

"Sorry...again. We don't have to go tonight." Elliot continued walking, gently brushing his hand up and down her back. Nervous flutters surrounded his heart as he waited for Lynn's response. She had been very quiet throughout the entire encounter. She probably thought he slept with Marybeth, which he never had. Nor ever would.

More silence. What was she thinking?

"I've never been with Marybeth. If you were wondering. I just don't want you to get the wrong impression. I'm sorry, Lynn."

She leaned into him, resting her head on his arm as they walked. "You have nothing to be sorry about. We can go to the party, if you want. If you're expected to go, then you should."

"I might be expected to go. I really did forget about the party. You distract me so easily. But I'm not going unless you go with me. Do you want to go?"

"It's been a long time since I went to a Christmas party. I'd love to go."

9

Gregory stood in the doorway while Lynn shuffled through the clothes in the closet. Happiness swooped in, filling his heart that he hadn't felt in a long time. He liked Lynn. He especially liked her for his son. Absolutely perfect for him. Thankfully, his son saw that as well.

Every year, Christmas approached with a doomed outlook. Worry came with it each time. Stress he shouldn't have, wondering if his son would see anything wonderful in front of him because Christmas was here, the blinders firmly affixed to his eyes. He never came out of his funk when the holidays rolled around.

Not this year. His son's smiles were brighter. Christmas music could be played in the house without low grumbles and the switch magically turned off. Presents filled the house. His son was finally letting the holiday spirit back in.

Lynn must've really made an impression on him. Having any sort of affection for a woman was rare as well. It tore his heart up that his son would never find happiness. Now it all seemed possible.

Perhaps now would be a good time to break the news to Elliot. He would be ready to handle it with Lynn here. He hoped so, anyway.

"So, what do you think, my dear?"

Lynn glanced at Gregory, a frown marring her beautiful features. "These are so lovely. I feel terrible wearing one of your wife's dresses to the party. It wouldn't be too much trouble for me to run home quickly and grab one of my own."

"Nonsense. My wonderful Abigail would've wanted you to wear one. The party starts in less than two hours. No sense in rushing. I'm glad you're coming along. It wasn't so difficult going to this when Abigail was here. She just loved mingling with everyone, passing along her infectious spirit. The first Christmas with just me and Elliot, I saw how miserable he was. He can hide his feelings well from everyone. I think this year he'll actually enjoy himself again, because of you."

"You honestly don't think Elliot will mind if I'm wearing one of these? Maybe we should wait for him to get back home." Lynn ran a hand down a green dress. "I'm sorry about your wife. I can see the pain in Elliot's eyes when he talks about her. She sounds like she was an amazing woman. I don't like seeing him unhappy."

Gregory stepped inside the room, one he generally didn't venture into because most of Abigail's belongings were in there. So painful at times.

He placed a tender hand on her shoulder. "She was the love of my life. She would have loved you. As soon as he gets back from the store picking up a pie and a bottle of wine for the party, he'll be knocked off his feet seeing you in this dress."

Gregory grabbed the green dress from the closet. He held it up, admiring the beauty of the dress and the way Lynn's eyes lit up at the prospect of wearing it. "I do believe you have your eye on this one. My beautiful Abigail, I don't think she ever wore it. She had this nasty habit of buying things, thinking she would use it or wear it or whatever her mind thought at the time. Half of these clothes she never wore. She loved shopping for clothes."

The dress hung in his hand, suddenly burning him straight to the gut. He swallowed to relieve the dryness in his throat and coughed. "You'd think it was Elliot who wanted to keep all of these things. He had such a hard time when she passed. It's me who refused to let him get rid of her stuff. Oh, we cleaned out a lot of her belongings, but there were just some things I couldn't part with. I can't even tell you why I kept the new clothes she never wore. Damn, I miss her."

Lynn smiled, taking the dress from his hands. "Laura's father, Trent, he died when she was a baby. In a car crash. You would think I would've been freaking out more when I crashed my car. Driving never makes me nervous, though. He was my rock, my savior, the only other person in the world I had. I still have some of his things. A small box tucked away in my closet that I take out now and again. And in the very, very back corner of my closet, I have a few shirts and his one nice suit. Every time I think about getting rid of them, I feel like a part of me will be gone as well. I understand perfectly what you're saying, Gregory. And for the first time in my life, I feel like it's not just Laura and me anymore. Elliot, and you, have reached into my heart taking quite a hold of it."

"Oh, you've grabbed my heart as well, Lynn. And Elliot,

well, I've never seen him happier than he is with you. So blessed that he met you." Gregory pulled her into a hug, squeezing delightfully. "Wear the green dress. I think Elliot will love it. I'll let you get ready."

Gregory smiled at her as he left the room.

Yes, that dress was perfect.

Perfect enough to distract his son from the blowing news he had.

Hopefully.

※

Lynn couldn't seem to hang the dress back up. Would it bother Elliot? It didn't seem to bother Gregory, his suggestion, really, that she wear the dress.

Going home would've been the wiser decision. She should've insisted harder. Why did any sort of smile from a Duncan man make her forget her side of the arguments? Gregory had that special power over her as well. Even though she desired to wear one of these beautiful dresses hanging in the closet, she should wear one of her own. Not that her dresses could compete with the ones in front of her. They couldn't. She would look like a rag doll if she showed up in one of her own.

The dress still hung in the air, her hands clutching the material with a death-like grip. Her feet were like lead. Moving toward the closet was impossible.

Gregory's words teetered back and forth. The green dress, slim and delicate, with a few beautiful glittering rhinestones on the front sparkled brightly. The elegance spoke to her. Enticed her.

Marybeth.

Ugh! Why would she think of her? She had been

pleasant enough when she met her. But perhaps she had been a little too friendly with Elliot.

Then he reassured her nothing ever occurred between them. And damn it, she had needed that reassurance. The smile and sultry words Marybeth had spoken had brought her insecurity front and center. She needed to look her best tonight, especially if she wanted to show Elliot she could look as sophisticated as Marybeth. She had felt very dowdy compared to her. Marybeth's hair had been perfectly styled in a beautiful coif, flawless makeup, and high heels that would've had Lynn falling flat on her face.

Lynn had tried to appear confident in front of her. Marybeth looked like a smart woman. She had probably seen nothing but a meek and mild woman. No competition for Elliot's affection.

Could there be some competition? How couldn't he want that woman? Lots of men probably liked Marybeth with her gorgeous looks and delicate body.

Apparently, Elliot knew better than that. Hopefully, anyway.

Wiping the doubt and insecurities away once again, she clutched the dress tighter and headed to the bathroom.

❄

"Do I look alright? Is my tie straight? What is she doing? Do you think she changed her mind?"

"Elliot, calm down. I haven't seen you this nervous since you took Sara O'Brian to the homecoming dance. She's beautifying herself like women do. She's just as nervous, so stop worrying. You two were meant for each other." Gregory straightened Elliot's tie.

"Meant for each other? You really think so, because I'm

really starting to think that. She surprised me with cookies today. Dad, I can't even tell you how that made me feel. No other woman I dated ever did anything thoughtful like that."

"She's wonderful, I agree. So don't screw it up."

Elliot frowned at his dad's back as he walked away. Don't screw it up? Shit! Was he screwing up somehow? Maybe he was pushing her too soon, wanting to spend so much time with her. Before he could continue his internal war of emotions, a sweet voice spoke from behind him.

"I'm ready. I hope you weren't waiting on me. I tried to get ready as quickly as possible."

Elliot turned around, his steady stance wobbling a little. Where was a chair to hold himself up when he needed it?

Absolutely exquisite. Dressed in a long green dress that personified her slender body, made him ache more than he ever had before. The top of the dress scooped into a lovely, graceful form, giving him just a hint of cleavage. It hugged her body all the way from her breasts to her thighs, where a small slit on the side gave him just a peek of her beautiful legs he always loved admiring. She wore a pair of silver high heels, just enough height to bring her to his level, but not high enough to tower over him. The shoes looked familiar, the dress a small hint of recognition as well. She sparkled like a rare emerald worth dying for.

"You hate it, I can just go—"

"No, Lynn. You're gorgeous. Shit, you have me standing here like a lovesick school boy," Elliot said, grabbing her hand before she could walk away.

He pulled her closer. His skin prickled with desire as all of the heat flowed straight below his belt. Devouring her from head to toe felt necessary. Like, now. Screw the party.

"This dress makes me want to peel it right off you and see what is underneath. The only reason I would hate it, is all the other men who will be gawking at you tonight. I'm not really looking forward to that. Let's stay home."

"So you like it?"

"Love it."

He kissed her neck, peppering small kisses to her ear. A tiny giggle erupted from her sweet lips as the sound of footsteps echoed in the air. Damn his dad for interrupting. He released a breath and shifted his body away from her. His pants were uncomfortably tight. Talk about embarrassing, but it clearly showed how much he truly loved the dress on her.

"Oh, Lynn, you look absolutely beautiful. My Abigail was a beauty, but I'm not sure the dress would've looked like that on her." Gregory smiled, his eyes glancing down at her feet. "Ah, I see her shoes fit you as well. What are the odds?"

"This is Mom's stuff? I thought the shoes looked familiar. I don't recall this dress, though." Elliot stood back, taking in his fill. Hard as a rock again. His pants were becoming more uncomfortable each time his eyes glossed over another part of her gorgeous body.

"If you don't like me wearing your mother's things, I can—"

"Stop. You look beautiful. My mother wouldn't mind." Elliot grabbed her hand and planted a light kiss. "I love this dress on you. You're wearing it. That's final."

"As I told Lynn, your mother never wore that dress. She bought it for, who knows what, and I kept it for...no clue. Obviously, for this special occasion." Gregory checked his watch, then glanced nervously at Elliot. "I should get going. I'll meet you two lovebirds at the party."

"Meet us? Why wouldn't you just drive with us?" Elliot asked.

"Well, I've been meaning to tell you. Now seems like a good time as any. I'm picking up my date, Gabby." Gregory fiddled with his tie.

Words failed him. Complete bafflement washed over him. "Date? As in, dating?" His dad shouldn't be dating anyone. It was wrong. All wrong.

"Yes, Elliot. She's a wonderful woman who makes me happy. I can't wait for you to meet her."

"I'm not sure I can say the same thing, Dad. What about Mom?"

"Don't speak to me that way, Elliot. Ever. I loved your mother and I always will. She's been gone three years, and she wouldn't want me to be unhappy. I'm not sure why you would." Gregory gave Lynn a smile as he walked toward the front door. "I'll see you at the party. I expect you to be polite to Gabby. Just fake it like you do concerning the holidays. You're good at it."

His dad closed the door with a quiet ease. What should have been a wonderful evening, alone with Lynn, instantly turned into a disaster. Definitely, screw the party.

A small, soft touch soothed his heart as Lynn squeezed his hand. "Are you okay, Elliot?"

"I just want to stay home with you and forget that conversation ever happened. He shouldn't be dating."

"Why not?"

Such a simple question, but loaded nonetheless. He whipped his eyes to her. Her concern reflected prominently. "Because he just shouldn't."

"Do you really want to stay home?" She rubbed a soft thumb over his hand, calming his heart even further. But how could he be calm when his father was dating someone?

"Elliot?"

"Yes, I want to stay home." He sighed heavily. "But we can't. My dad will know why we didn't show. Plus, I'm the chief of police, it's sort of expected I go to this party. Most of the town council members will be there, the mayor, and anyone else who thinks they're important. They'll all wonder why I didn't show if I bail out."

"I'll go grab my purse from the bedroom." She kissed him lightly on the lips. "Elliot, maybe I'm overstepping my boundaries, but why is it so wrong for your father to be happy? He didn't want to tell you about this new woman. You could see how nervous he was, probably because he knew how you'd react. Didn't you see it? He truly cares for this woman. Give her a chance."

"Why should I? What about my mother? He's just going to throw that love away."

Elliot dropped her hand and turned around. Taking her comfort and being angry at the same time wouldn't work. She didn't do anything wrong, but her words hurt. His dad shouldn't be dating anyone. Period. End of story.

"Just because he's seeing someone new doesn't mean he's throwing her love away. He spoke to me earlier about her, and I could hear the love, the longing to see her once again. But he's moving on with his life because she's not here anymore. I know how he feels."

Elliot glanced back at her, his brows dipping with confusion. "What?"

"I told you about Trent. You know what he meant to me. He still holds a place in my heart. I would never throw his love away, but I can make room for a bit more love. If I wasn't willing to make room for another man, do you think I'd be here in this room with you right now? Do you think I would've ever given you a chance? If you think your father shouldn't have the chance to be happy with another woman, then maybe I shouldn't give you a chance either. It's the same thing."

She left him standing there speechless. God, what was she saying? More words he didn't want to hear. His father was dating and it sounded like he was on the verge of losing Lynn.

Don't screw it up.

Boy, those words held so much meaning now. Because that's exactly what he was doing. Screwing everything up. As much as he wanted to ignore what she said, her words held a ring of truth. She lost someone she deeply loved and decided to give him a chance after how many years of being alone. Why couldn't his dad do the same thing?

Because it hurt. Hearing those words from his dad had swiftly ripped his heart from his chest with one giant punch. His dad wanted him to give this woman a chance. How could he? Did that truly mean he'd lose Lynn if he didn't?

They left a few minutes later for the party. The silence that filled the truck crumbled Elliot's heart into tiny pieces. Putting it all back together seemed nearly impossible. Since the moment she spoke those words, it's like she slipped further and further away from him. He was going to lose her. The first time he felt a moment of true happiness, just to be ripped away without effort. It would be all his fault.

Small talk seemed futile. What could he say to gain reassurance he wouldn't lose her? Nothing short of accepting this woman into his life would work. So he stayed quiet, just as she did. He would lose her. And why? Because his dad wanted to live out the rest of his life with someone else. To have a bit of happiness since his mom died.

Hurting his father again. Something he was obviously

good at. And with potential health concerns. He hadn't seen any other signs of forgetfulness, but that didn't mean he didn't worry about it. His dad still loved his mom. He knew this. He saw it all the time in the little things his dad did or said.

Damn, Lynn was right. She was gone and his dad had to move on. Accepting that and living with it would be hard. How could he do that without his heart breaking into a million pieces?

By the time they reached the party and stepped into the ballroom, a smile appeared on his face as if nothing had happened.

Faking it.

Just like his dad said he could do with ease. Shame swamped his bones, but it didn't stop him from replacing his smile with a frown. Nope. His smile shined brightly as he laughed with everyone, talked with enthusiasm, and grinned as if he hadn't had a care in the world. To his surprise, Lynn appeared just as happy alongside him. It looked as if they were a new couple, happy, no problems between them. That couldn't be farther from the truth.

Lynn excused herself to use the bathroom. The hint of pain in her eyes before she walked away tore him up. The first sign that she really wasn't happy or enjoying herself.

Faking it.

Obviously, she knew how to do it as well.

She loved Christmas. This party was supposed to make her happy. Truly happy. Not this sham they were both putting on.

Getting out of the house to enjoy such an extravagant party during the holidays probably didn't happen very often for her. Every year, everyone always dressed in their finest clothes, wore the best jewelry they owned, and if they were special enough, received an invitation to the Christmas party. City officials, the Mayor, prominent businessmen and women from around the town and surrounding areas, even Senator Barkins attended the party, especially since he grew up in Mulberry. For such a small town, it was an honor to be invited. A tradition that had been going strong for the last thirty years. Another reason he couldn't miss the blasted party.

The ballroom, located in the oldest hotel in town that held the party every year, had been decorated beautifully. White Christmas lights were strung around the room, giving off an elegant appearance. A big tree that sat centered in the middle of the room, stood out brightly with its colorful arrangements of lights, ornaments, and presents sitting under the tree. Lynn's eyes had lit up by all of the presents under the tree. Everyone came with a gift in tow, placing it under the tree. He informed her they would be delivered tomorrow to the children at the hospital in Mulberry and the surrounding areas. Another beautiful smile had graced her features. Another reason for him to like Christmas again.

She grumbled a tiny bit he didn't tell her about donating a gift. She would've donated as well. Of course. That sounded just like her. Not that she told him specifically, but he knew money was tight. None of that mattered to her. She was a loving, giving person. He had donated two gifts, one from him and one from her. Although, he didn't specify that to her. No need for another argument to ensue.

He loved seeing her enthusiasm for the holiday. So why did the night have to start out the way it had? Or continue on the way it was?

She was so damn beautiful. He certainly wasn't having

fun watching some of the men and the way they looked at her. They all could see her beauty, her sweetness. Would her attention be drawn to another man in the room? Would he lose her completely before the night ended?

Clenching his fists, he relaxed them gradually and shoved his hands into his pockets when his dad, and the woman he assumed was Gabby, made a path straight to him. Where was Lynn? Why was she taking so long in the bathroom? He needed her here, now, more than ever. She calmed him. Brought him peace like nothing else.

"Elliot, we've been trying to make our way to you and Lynn the entire night. It's just so busy. So many people to say hello to. Where's Lynn?" Gregory asked as if nothing was wrong between them.

"She had to use the restroom. She should be right back." Elliot glimpsed at the woman next to his dad. She wore a gold-colored evening gown that fit her perfectly. It showed her elegance, yet dissuaded her age to make her appear younger. She had fine wrinkles lining her eyes as she smiled at him. Short, white hair styled in light waves that made her look lovelier than what brown or black or even blonde hair would've made her look. While she would never look more beautiful than his mother, she had a beautiful quality to her that he could appreciate.

"Well, I'd like you to meet Gabby. Gabby, this is my son, Elliot."

His father's hand trembled as he pointed during the introduction. More shame consumed him. His father was worried he'd make a scene, or at least, say something rude. Talk about being a horrible son.

He produced a genuine smile as he held out a hand. "Nice to meet you, Gabby. I'm afraid my dad hasn't told me much about you because I've been in my own little world regarding Lynn. We just started dating. I guess I'm still in the butterfly stage where my nerves take over and all I think about is her."

"Gregory pointed you and Lynn out in the crowd and I can see why your mind is distracted. She's beautiful. It's a pleasure to meet you, Elliot. Gregory talks about you all the time." Gabby shook his hand, placing a soft hand over their clasped hands. "He also talks about your mother. She sounds like she was a wonderful woman. I wish I could have met her. I miss my Phillip every day."

"Phillip?" Elliot inquired as she finally let go of his hand. Amazing. She had managed to calm his heart a little. Just like Lynn.

"My late husband. I'm a widow as well. I was a bit lost at first, leaning towards the church for comfort. That's where I met Gregory. He fills my days with happiness again," she said, nudging his shoulder.

Gregory placed an arm around her, squeezing her with delight. He looked at Elliot, gratefulness pouring from his eyes.

Well, at least he wasn't still screwing things up. No matter what he felt moments before when he shook Gabby's hand, he needed some space. And where was Lynn? She had been gone a long time.

"Maybe I should check on Lynn."

"Why don't I check on her for you? You can't exactly walk into the women's restroom, can you?" Gabby said with a small chuckle.

"No, I suppose not."

She walked away before he could argue with her. He had wanted to check on Lynn. He had wanted to escape.

"So what do you think?"

"I think I acted like a jerk, Dad. She seems nice. Can we

talk about it later?" He ran a hand through his hair. No escaping his dad. Always straight and to the point. "I really am worried about Lynn. We sort of argued. She was on your side about Gabby. It felt like she gave me an ultimatum while trying to get me to see how much of an idiot I am."

"An ultimatum? She doesn't seem like the type. Maybe you misunderstood her." Gregory placed a hand on Elliot's shoulder. "I never wanted you two to argue over something like this. I'm sorry if I surprised you with the news. I've wanted to tell you for a while now. I just didn't know how. Your mother will always have a place in my heart. I did it tonight, well, because I had to since Gabby is my date for the party. But also, because I thought Lynn being there would help soften the blow. I'm sorry if you're fighting because of me. That wasn't my intention."

"I just have to keep the faith that I can fix this. I just hope she's not hiding in the bathroom because of me."

Gregory squeezed his shoulder a bit. "Maybe she just got caught in some conversation. I think I saw Marybeth walk toward the bathroom when we were making our way to you."

"You did? I'll be right back, Dad."

Elliot walked away. Marybeth hadn't acted that horrible in front of them earlier today, but Elliot wasn't immune to how vicious she could be. She was a spoiled brat who always got her way with a snap of her fingers to her father. Just one more reason he didn't want to date her. High maintenance. He didn't need that sort of woman in his life.

He needed Lynn. What were the odds they were having a nice conversation about the party? He didn't know how much more Lynn could take. So much for having a sleepover.

He resisted the urge to shove people out of his way as he

rushed through the throng of people. She would surely hate him if Marybeth said anything to suggest there was something going on between them.

Losing Lynn would be like losing his heart completely. And hating Christmas until the end of time.

10

Lynn stepped out of the stall and smoothed her dress down with trembling hands. The last thing she needed was to create wrinkles in such a lovely dress. The tension between her and Elliot was enough to worry about.

By all indications, the evening wouldn't be ending like she had hoped this morning. Falling helplessly into Elliot's arms. Paying him back for fixing her car seemed even more crucial now. She would walk away from this small-lived relationship without being indebted to him.

The brown box faded in many spots that sat tucked away in her closet squeezed at her gut again. She hadn't opened it in months. Taking out Trent's things, even after all this time, could put her in a serious funk. Laura didn't need to see that.

Now, her choices were slim. She would have to take it out when she got home. The thought of removing the one thing that would cure her money problems made her steps wobble as she walked to the sink. The pain of losing him would happen all over again.

So much pain.

Sniffling, she swiped a hand across her cheek, erasing the only tear she would shed. No more. Crying would just make the night worse.

Yanking on the faucet, the water flowing freely, she washed her hands. Too bad the water couldn't wash her problems away as well.

While the tension swirled around her and Elliot, she had enjoyed the evening somewhat. The festivities of Christmas always filled her soul with happiness. Knowing Elliot wasn't happy dimmed that happiness immensely. Ending the evening would probably be best. Just end it all.

She had nobody to blame but herself. She had to throw out those damaging words to him. How could she know anything about the relationship between him and his father? What made her such an expert on relationships?

She knew how it felt to love someone so special, then lose them in a blink of an eye. She had seen Gregory's pain when he spoke about his late wife. She had also seen the happiness when he mentioned Gabby. She could relate to both of those feelings. She felt pain when she thought of Trent, and she felt happiness when she thought of Elliot. That's all she had really been trying to tell him.

Drying her hands slowly didn't diminish the rapid beating of her heart. How would Elliot react when she asked to go home? Immediately agree with her or convince her to stay? He probably didn't want to continue seeing her after she opened her mouth the way she had. He might even be grateful she wanted to go home. Gregory was right. Elliot could fake happiness very well, yet, the sadness in his eyes never wavered since they walked out of his house. Of course, nobody seemed to notice. She did. She had from the start.

She tossed the paper towels into the trash receptacle near the faucet and turned around.

"Oh, Marybeth. Hello. How are you?"

Marybeth smiled, her eyes twinkling with mischief. Could she actually see the tension between her and Elliot? Did she know something Lynn didn't?

"I'm wonderful. How is your evening going, Gwynn?"

Her eyebrow slowly rose. Intentional, or accidental? "It's Lynn. And I've been having a wonderful evening as well."

"My apologies. I swore Elliot said Gwynn earlier. How long have you been dating?"

"A while. I'll leave you to it."

Lynn smiled even as the pain in her heart swelled. Marybeth looked absolutely flawless, once again, in her evening gown that clung to her body with ease. Had Elliot seen her yet this evening?

"Are you breaking up with Elliot?"

Lynn jerked as she took a step forward. She pointed toward the stalls. "I meant going to the bathroom. That's all. I get the impression you like him."

"I think it's mutual, actually. I'm so sorry he seems to be leading you on. I hate to say anything, but sometimes it's easier to know sooner rather than later."

"Leading me on?" Marybeth was wrong. Elliot would never do anything like that.

Marybeth shook her head as her lips curled with delight. "You're so innocent. It's kind of sad. Look at me and then look at yourself. You'll clearly see why Elliot would want me instead. No disrespect, but you probably purchased that dress at a thrift store, where I'm sure you get all your clothes, don't you? Elliot's used to the finer things in life."

The audacity of this woman. She had suspected she liked Elliot, but Lynn never expected her to be so cruel.

"As a matter of fact, I do. It helps me save money. I work hard to earn money. Do you even know what working hard means?"

"I know Elliot's leading you on. I'm just trying to help you see that. Don't take it personally. You should be grateful."

Lynn's jaw almost dropped, yet snapped it shut as she clenched her teeth. Déjà vu. It's like her mother was standing right in front of her. She hadn't seen her in years, and she had no intention of wanting to see her in the future. Interacting with a woman who reminded her of her mother wasn't something she wanted to deal with either.

"I'd be grateful to end this conversation. That's about it. Excuse me, Marybeth."

"Gwynn, I didn't mean to upset you."

"It's Lynn. I don't appreciate you making Elliot look like a horrible person. You say he's leading me on. The man I know would never do such a thing. He's kind, generous, and smart enough not to date you. Please, Marybeth, don't take that personally. I'm just trying to help you see that."

Marybeth backed up a step, clearly surprised. "You have no idea what you're talking about. Elliot likes me. His eyes have been telling me that all night. He can't seem to stop daring a glance. Has he even commented on that dress you're wearing? Honestly, I'm starting to feel a little sorry for you now."

Delusional, or clearly persistent? Trying to make heads or tails of her behavior wouldn't get her anywhere. They could probably go back and forth all night in this bathroom.

"Let's get something straight. It doesn't bother me to wear thrift clothes. I can still look as glamorous as you in them. Money isn't everything. And for your information, this is his mother's dress. I dare you to tell him just exactly what you think of it. Because if you know anything at all about Elliot, you know what his mother meant to him. I think this conversation has reached its limit. Excuse me."

She believed Elliot when he said he never had anything to do with Marybeth. And now she understood why. Good for him for seeing the train wreck she clearly was.

She took a few steps, stopping when Marybeth refused to move out of the way. Freedom was just a pull of the door. Blocked. "Move, please."

"Gwynn, I don't think you understand."

Lynn leaned forward, getting inches from her face. "It's Lynn, for the last time. And I don't think you understand. I'll push you out of the way if I have to. I want to leave this restroom."

"Gosh, and I won't hesitate to scream assault." Marybeth cocked her head as a wide smirk spread across her face.

Lynn screamed loudly. Marybeth jumped back. A chuckled escaped as she grabbed the door handle. "You must be really lonely. Why else would you be so cruel? Merry Christmas, Marybeth. I truly don't want to fight with you. This should be a joyous time of year."

Lynn exited the bathroom with the hopes Marybeth left her alone for the rest of the night. With the tension between her and Elliot, she couldn't help but worry that Marybeth might swoop in and snatch him away. Would Elliot do that to her?

No. She believed him. He didn't like Marybeth.

"Oh, geez, I'm so sorry. I don't know where my mind is at," Lynn said as she almost collided with another woman.

"Probably still fighting that woman inside the bathroom," the woman said with a laugh.

Lynn's eyes rounded with shock. "Did you hear what was said? I didn't mean—"

"Oh, dear, you didn't say anything horrible. I sure hope that wasn't an apology about to leave your mouth. I heard some of the conversation. I'm Gabby, by the way." She held her hand out in greeting.

"Gregory's Gabby?"

"Oh, I like the sound of that. Yes, I am." Gabby laughed as Lynn shook hands with her. "You must be Elliot's Lynn."

"Yes, I am. Or, I hope so." She laughed without enthusiasm as she brushed her hands down her dress.

"Why would you sound so unsure? I just met him, but he seemed quite concerned about you. He was about to walk into this bathroom himself, until I suggested it would be better if I did."

"We, uh, didn't exactly see eye-to-eye on an issue before we left for the party. What can I say? I'm a little worried."

"I don't think you have anything to worry about. What was the issue?"

"Uh, well...it's okay. I'm sure we'll work it out." Lynn gestured her hand. "Perhaps we should join Elliot and Gregory now."

"Yes, of course."

Worry. That's all the night had held. Lynn wasn't about to start another problem by mentioning the reason her and Elliot were having issues. How would Gabby take the news? Best not to find out. And hurting Gregory in that manner wasn't on her to-do list. One Duncan man angry with her was enough.

Escaping this party became crucial. Gabby could have more questions later. Elliot would continue to pretend to enjoy himself when he clearly wasn't. And taking the chance of another encounter with Marybeth would be too much. She had enough.

"Lynn, there you are. Is everything okay?" Elliot asked as he rounded the corner.

Just seeing his face brought a smile. Yet, the worry still lingered, especially the way he looked flushed. His words were a bit breathless. Concern immediately took front and center. "Everything's fine. I was just meeting Gabby. Are you okay?"

"Of course, but you had me worried when you were gone so long. My dad's probably waiting for us. Let's join him." Elliot held out his arm to Lynn.

Her smile widened at the eagerness in his expression. His soft touch, no matter how small, always helped to calm her down. Nothing to worry about. Maybe the night wouldn't have to end so soon. His concern for her couldn't be misinterpreted. Always so much concern. He really did worry too much about things. Perhaps she was worrying too much about the strain between them.

She took a step, then stumbled as Marybeth rushed past her and grasped Elliot's arm. Great. Now what was she up to?

"Oh, Elliot, there you are. I...I don't know what to say," Marybeth said between shaky breaths.

Elliot's brows dipped in confusion, sparing a worried glance at Lynn. "What are you talking about?"

Marybeth tilted her eyes to Lynn, her lips barely curling, but enough to see the devious glint. "Your girlfriend and I had some words in the restroom. Just out of nowhere, she was telling me to back off. I have no idea what I did to cause such a reaction from her. And she muttered under her breath before that, how much she hated her dress. It's such a lovely dress. I'm not sure why she'd wear it if she didn't like it. And then I tried to leave the restroom and she pushed me."

Elliot looked back and forth between Marybeth and Lynn. Her stomach dropped as his face contorted with anger. He was always such a friendly, loving man. Anger never made an appearance, even in their small arguments. He always managed to keep a smile on his face. Probably the reason she always let the arguments drop. That sweet smile of his.

Now, nothing but anger. Why did it seem directed at her?

The nerve of this woman. Such a master with words. Her mother's face flashed before her again. Escaping the past always caught up to a person somehow. Tears started to pool in the corner of her eyes.

Gabby's hand brushed her arm, offering her comfort. So she saw his anger as well. What a disastrous night.

"Elliot—"

He refused to look at her as he cut her off, his attention solely focused on Marybeth. "What is the matter with you, Marybeth? I have a hard time believing everything you just said. Lynn loves that dress. If she didn't like it, she would've said so because she's an honest person." Elliot shook her hand off and backed up a step.

"Elliot, she pushed me. I want to press charges. You're the chief of police, you can't ignore that." Marybeth crossed her arms as she pouted her lips.

"I don't think she pushed you. I was right outside the bathroom door. If anything, I heard Lynn scream. Did she touch you, Lynn?" Gabby said, looking at Lynn with concern.

Elliot's head frantically whipped to Lynn, the concern just as prominent. "Did she hurt you?"

"Elliot, she pushed me. Why are you ignoring me?" Marybeth demanded.

Lynn ignored Marybeth's tantrum. Acting the way her seven year old could act, rarely, but it did happen. Such desperation. Perhaps Marybeth could finally see that Elliot didn't want her.

"No, she didn't. She refused to move out of my way, so I screamed, which made her jump back. I never touched her and she never touched me."

Lynn wrapped her arms around herself. Could she ward off all the unhappiness surrounding them? She had wanted to enjoy a nice, wonderful Christmas party. Instead, they had to deal with this.

"Elliot, I—"

"Oh, stop it, Marybeth Jenkins. Move on from Chief Duncan. He clearly has his eyes on another woman. Just because your father is on the City Council does not give you the right to treat others with disrespect. Chief Duncan, nobody touched anybody in the restroom. I was in one of the stalls and heard it all. If you'd like to arrest somebody, I suggest arresting Marybeth Jenkins for a false report," City Councilwoman Tina Waters said with quiet decorum.

"And you, Lynn, stood up for yourself quite admirably. Well done. I hope you don't let this ruin the rest of your evening," Tina said, looking at her with a brilliant smile.

"I certainly wouldn't have gotten anywhere in life if I let people bring me down," Lynn softly replied.

"Come, Marybeth, join me. I think if you walk away now, Chief Duncan will decide to forgo pressing charges for a false report. Right, Chief?" Tina said.

"I think I could manage that." Elliot walked over to Lynn, grabbing her hand. Peace descended immediately, her heart filling back up with serenity. "But I hope this doesn't happen again. I won't be so forgiving next time."

"Of course not. I wouldn't either." Tina smiled brightly

as she steered Marybeth out of the room, who looked ready to explode that the situation didn't go her way.

"Well, that was certainly more entertainment than I bargained for at this party. I'll go find Gregory and meet up with you two later." Gabby smiled gently before walking away.

Lynn trembled as Elliot blew out a breath. He brought her hand to his mouth and lightly kissed it. A few more trembles escaped. His soft touch could still heat her up without much effort.

"I'm sorry, Lynn. I had no idea Marybeth could act that way. To accuse you of something like that...I just can't understand her. What did she say in there?"

"It doesn't matter."

"I want to know."

"Don't worry about it. Let's just forget it. Let's forget it all." Lynn glanced down at his chest. His warm touch had calmed her down, but his eyes could tell a completely different story. Could they still salvage what they had between them? An apology for opening her mouth earlier concerning his dad and Gabby was a good place to start.

"Forget it all? Why do I feel like I'm losing you?" Elliot asked, pulling her hand closer to his chest, making her move closer as well.

God, she needed his arms around her. To pull her close and take the pain away. Take the worry away.

"I'm sorry about what I said at the house. It's your dad, and I shouldn't have said anything."

"It might take me a while to warm up to the idea, but I think it'll be easier with you by my side." He grabbed her face, his heartache pouring from his eyes. "You didn't answer me. Am I losing you?"

"No."

His hands slid down her sides and wove around to her back. Exactly what she wanted him to do.

"That's all I needed to hear. Do you want to leave?"

She shook her head as his warm touch started to soothe her. "Let's enjoy this party."

Elliot smiled. He wrapped her even tighter in his arms and dove in for a kiss. A deep, fierce kiss that spoke volumes. The worry slowly ebbed away.

"So we're still on for our sleepover?"

Lynn leaned into him, whispering into his ear delicately, "I've been looking forward to it. Maybe I am ready to leave."

11

Lynn let out a soft, silent breath. Nerves. Nearly thirty years old and the nerves could still appear out of nowhere. A woman with a seven-year-old daughter. She knew how sex operated. What was there to be nervous about? Nothing would happen she didn't want to. Oh, but she wanted every little thing to happen between her and Elliot.

The tension filling the car said a lot would happen once they reached his house. Sexual tension, that is. None of that other stress remained. Maybe the air could be cleared a little better, but tomorrow would work. Tonight, the heat she always experienced by a simple glance from him or a tender word from his sweet mouth or even the littlest contact from him would be extinguished. No more needing cold air to cool her down.

Maybe. One time with him might not be enough.

One worry at a time. They still had to get through their first time in one piece. God, it had been so long. Her infrequent occasional dates meant nothing. She hadn't slept with a man since Trent.

The butterflies fluttering around her stomach were going crazy. Almost like it was her first time. How bad would she screw this up? This could be the most pivotal moment in their short relationship.

Very short. She had never contemplated sleeping with a man so soon before. With Elliot, it just felt right. How had she gone so long without a man in her bed? Probably because none of those men had been Elliot.

Nothing to it. She could do this. Just pull all of those wily ways of seduction out and work some magic.

Ugh! She never seduced a man. Not even Trent. More like he swooped into her life, mastered the charm like a pro and made her fall completely in love without blinking an eye.

Elliot was almost doing the same exact thing.

Another breath released. No worries.

Not even the last hour at the party had held any worries. They had stuck by his father and Gabby. And Gabby was a remarkable woman. She couldn't remember either of her grandmothers that well, since they died when Lynn was a young child, but Gabby reminded her of how a grandmother would be. Someone she could turn to in a time of need, or someone who would lend an ear, or even someone she could spend the day with simply enjoying each other's company. An instant connection had sparked between them. She could see why Gregory liked her.

Whether it was her by his side, or the realization sinking in better, but Elliot had remained friendly, asking polite questions as if he truly cared about Gabby's response. He had held her hand most of the time. A few trembles had escaped every once in a while. He didn't want to let another woman into his father's life, but he was trying. That told her just what kind of man he was.

Besides everything that had happened, she had a wonderful time at the party. While the party consisted mostly of the upper class in the town of Mulberry, they treated it like a party at someone's home. She loved that part the most. Everyone brought a gift for under the tree, and some people, like Elliot, contributed to the food, sort of like a potluck. Nobody looked down at her like she didn't belong. Everyone greeted her with a friendly smile and eagerness to know more about her, especially when they saw Elliot's arm around her.

"Long thoughts over there. We're almost home. Did you want to try calling Laura?" Elliot asked, reaching for her hand that rested on her lap.

"No, she would call if she had a problem. I'm glad you didn't mind I gave your number to Ashley's mom in case she needed me. I should get with the times and get a cell phone. It's just...well, I'm old-fashioned." That excuse sounded better than the actual truth. She was poor and couldn't afford a cell phone.

Elliot kissed her hand, keeping it on his lap as he continued to drive home. The fireworks were already starting. "Did you enjoy the party? I'm sorry again about Marybeth."

"I had a wonderful time, Elliot. Let's forget about all that other stuff."

He kissed her hand again, his lips lingering before he set her hand back down on his lap. His kiss told her just what he was thinking about.

She smiled. The shivers wracking her body could be interpreted in so many ways. Nerves. Desire ramping up. More nerves. "I want to spend the night, but what will your dad think?" *You are not making excuses because you're scared. You are not making excuses.*

"Well, not that I really want to think about that. I really, really don't, actually. But my dad informed me before we left that he wouldn't be home tonight. Regardless, my dad wouldn't mind. We're adults, Lynn. Plus, it's my house." He grinned at her with that last statement.

"Your house or not, he's your dad."

"True, but if you haven't noticed, he adores you. He wouldn't care."

❈

A BRIGHT RED ribbon with sparkling snowflakes punched him in the gut. Why in the world would the thought of that present pop into his head?

A sign maybe. The only reason he met her in the first place. Should he tell her about that? Once they got home, their relationship would move into a whole new level. Having that present between them might not be a good thing. How would she react?

A very proud woman. So thoughtful, giving, caring. Her reaction could be very bad. He almost lost her earlier tonight over his own stupidity and over Marybeth's interference. He couldn't lose her. Not yet. The ache below his belt and in his heart needed this one night with her at least.

"Your hand is shaking. Does that mean you're just as nervous as me?"

He quickly looked down at their hands linked. How had he let that happen? Projecting his nervousness. "I'm sitting next to a beautiful woman, who I'm dying to have the minute I get home. Maybe I'm a little nervous. Do you know what you mean to me, Lynn?"

"I can guess. How did I get so lucky to meet you?"

It's like she read his mind. Spill the beans. Tell her about the present. Come clean how he had been searching for the owner of a present that should've never landed on his doorstep, but very thankful that it had.

Christmas socks. Oh, the delicious things he could do with those. Take each one, slowly caress her leg as he put them on her. And only the socks. She had to be completely naked in just the socks.

"Elliot? You look a little flushed."

He cleared his throat and squeezed her hand in reassurance. "Just thinking too many thoughts of what I want to do with you when we get home. And thankfully, we're home."

Nope. Not a good time to tell her. Tonight was his night. The damn present could wait until tomorrow.

He pulled into the driveway and shut off the truck. No more thinking about the present. That wasn't important right now. Showing her what she meant to him was the most important thing. He needed a plan of attack before he confessed his sins. Because when he finally told her the truth, losing her wasn't an option.

"Why are we nervous? We've both done this before." He chuckled, gaining a sweet smile from her.

"It's been a long time for me, Elliot. I just want it to be perfect."

"You are perfect. And it's been a while for me, too. Can I take you in the house now and ravish you?"

She giggled. "Please do."

The wind swirled around, biting into his cheeks, yet all he could feel was the warmth of desire standing beside him.

He shoved open the door and pulled her eagerly inside out of the cold. He helped her out of her coat, brushing his fingers along her shoulders before hanging it up next to his coat in the closet. He removed his suit jacket, laying it gently over the small table near the door, then flipped the lock on the door and took off his shoes. As soon as she had carefully taken her heels off, he backed her into the wall near the closet, kissing her with a desired frenzy.

His tongue mingled with hers, tasting the wonderful flavor of the cookies she had nibbled on at the party before they left. He tenderly bit her lip, trailing soft kisses from her neck to her ear, taking his time with each kiss. Getting to know every part of her body.

"I want you, Lynn. I could take you right here against this wall. Hell, in every spot in my house. I want to mark you as mine. Say you're mine." He sucked on her earlobe as he moved his hands from her hips to her back.

"I'm all yours, Elliot. Take me anywhere you want."

His hands slid up her back, finding the zipper to her dress. He pulled down with slow precision and let the dress drop to the floor. As he stepped back to drink in the sight of her wondrous body, his knees buckled as the intensity of his need skyrocketed.

"You've been completely naked under this dress all night? You are so lucky I didn't know this before we left." He delivered a delicious grin as she bit her lip with enticement. Every curve of her just waiting for his soft touch. No panties, no bra to contend with. Yet, he stood frozen.

"And just what would've you done? I would love to know." She smiled artfully, smoothing her hands down his chest and pulled his shirt out from inside his pants. Her fingers trailed a burning path. She slowly started to unbutton each button and all he could do was stare at the longing in her eyes. Her fingers brushed his skin every time she unhooked a button. "Speechless? I'm surprised."

He grazed over her entire body as her fingers continued to create magic with each delicate brush. He had no words. He just wanted to soak it all in. She reached the last button, loosened his tie, and tossed the tie and shirt to the ground. She stroked his chest with a sweet caress, taking her time to touch every curve. He released a sigh when she unbuckled his belt and unzipped his pants. Her hand slid inside and finally reached its mark.

His turn.

He pushed her against the wall, whispering hoarsely against her mouth, "I would've done this." He crushed his mouth to hers, his entire body pressing against her as the heat rose between them.

Her soft body molded perfectly with his. This wasn't how he imagined their first time, but it suddenly felt right. No protest slipped from her lips. Only sweet moans of delight as he grinded against her. He needed her. And he needed her now.

He tangoed with her, the kiss intensifying as he reached into his back pocket, fumbling in his wallet until the smooth condom packet hit his fingers. He dropped his wallet to the floor at the same time his pants fell. He covered himself quickly.

Without once breaking the kiss, he lifted her up, and slowly let her sink down onto him. He moaned into her mouth, then kissed her cheek. "Shit, I might not last long. You feel so damn good."

"We have all night, Elliot. You're supposed to stay up really late at a sleepover, aren't you?" Small kisses peppered his neck as he started to rock her up and down, loving her sweetly against the wall.

"I plan to keep you up for a very long time."

He claimed her mouth again, continuing the sweet assault against her body. He clutched her hips tighter as he pulled in and out of her with a delightful hunger. His fingers itched to learn, memorize every inch of her body, play tenderly with her breasts, glide further down and make the magic hotter, but he only held her firmly to the wall.

Before long, his pleasure became too much as she started to squeeze the life right out of him, her climax hitting with intensity. Her body shuddered in bliss. His passion swept away with her as the love between them wrapped around his heart and staked permanent claim.

He loved this woman. That simple. No reservations. No hesitations. Just love. He didn't ask for a gift this Christmas, but he received the best one out there.

He bit his tongue before the words fell out. Not yet. There was only one way he could tell her. It would give him plenty of time to plan the perfect setting.

He buried his head into her neck as his breaths came out heavily, just as deeply as hers. She had to have felt the same magic as him. Her body told him so.

"Now, we're going to take it slowly. I'm going to cover every inch of this gorgeous body with my lips. Any objections?" he whispered into her ear.

"None. I'm all yours."

That's all he needed to hear.

He carried her to the bedroom where he continued to show her just how much he loved her. There wasn't one part of her body he didn't kiss, caress, and love with sweet devotion. Before they fell into a peaceful sleep, she mumbled in his ear about their clothes scattered in the foyer. What happened if his dad came home before they could pick everything up?

That really hadn't crossed his mind, not that he would have cared either. But he dragged his butt out of bed to grab their clothes and jumped back in with renewed energy. She glided into his embrace with ease, and with as much anticipation as him. They loved each other one more time before they fell into a deep sleep.

They slept late into the morning, not once letting the sun wake them from their quiet slumber.

A loud, piercing sound jolted Elliot awake. He blinked a few times before it registered it was his phone ringing on his nightstand.

He grabbed the phone, mumbling a brief hello. His eyes shot open when the concerned woman's voice on the other end identified herself.

"Yes, she's right here. Hold on a minute." Elliot covered the phone slightly, nudging Lynn lightly on the shoulder. "Sweetheart, wake up. It's Ashley's mom."

Lynn shifted under the covers, but didn't open her eyes. He leaned closer, placing a light kiss on her cheek. The small amount of sunlight streaming in haloed her face like an angel. Oh, how he could've woke her up in a completely different way.

"Lynn, sweetheart, you need to wake up. You have a phone call. It concerns Laura."

Lynn perked up at the sound of her daughter's name. "What time is it? What's wrong?"

"It's a little after ten," Elliot said, glancing at the clock on the nightstand. "Ashley's mom didn't say what was wrong, just asked for you. She sounded slightly panicked."

Worry instantly punctured her face. He could relate to that. Worry had started to worm its way inside the moment Ashley's voice echoed with panic. He loved Lynn, which meant he loved Laura as well.

She grabbed the phone from him, spitting out question after question. A few minutes later, she hung up the phone.

"Is she okay? Talk to me." He pulled her closer, their hearts beating rapidly in tune. This was what it felt like to be a worried parent. He didn't care how little he had known Lynn and her daughter. Laura felt like his child already. Damn, he loved that little girl just as much as he loved Lynn. He would do anything to help with whatever the issue happened to be.

"Laura broke her arm. My baby's in pain and I'm not there. I'm not there, Elliot."

Tears started to fall down. He gently grabbed her chin, wiping the tears away. "Hey, it's okay. We'll get dressed and head to the hospital right away. Everything will be fine. Did she say how it happened?"

"Playing in the snow. They were sledding and she wiped out pretty badly. She could have more injuries than that."

He brushed a finger over her lips. "You don't know that. Let's get dressed and go to the hospital. She said a broken arm, that's it. Don't think any more bad thoughts."

"You'll drop me off?"

He cradled her face and leaned in closer, his lips almost touching hers. "Let's get something straight. I'm not just dropping you off. I'm staying with you until you leave the hospital, and even after that, I won't leave your side. We'll get through this mishap together. Like we will with all future endeavors. I told you I wanted it all, which means, I'm here for it all. Every single little thing that happens. Laura means a great deal to me as well. Not just you. Do you hear me?"

"I'm just so scared. She's never broken a bone before. I feel like a terrible mother not being there."

"You're a wonderful mother. We'll be scared together. I won't leave your side."

He kissed her briefly, then produced a tender smile. "You know my aversion to hospitals. But for you and Laura, I'll do anything."

12

Elliot gently sat down on the couch and handed Laura a mug. "Hot chocolate. My mom used to make this for me when I wasn't feeling well. I'm not a pro like she was, but I tried."

Laura raised her lips into a sweet smile. "I'm a one-handed monster now. I hope I don't spill it."

She grabbed the mug by the handle with her right hand. Her left arm was cradled in a long cast that reached from her hand past her elbow. Bright pink adorned the outside with a few signatures already scattered around. The task of picking a color at the hospital had taken a while. Pink's her favorite color, but the pain and fear of getting her arm wrapped had been a little too much for her. Elliot had wanted to pull her close and take all the pain and sadness away. Sort of like right now.

"More like a one-handed munchkin. I spilled my coffee last week over by that chair in the corner. I set it on the floor and just forgot it was there when I stood up. Water and a rag. That's all it takes to wipe up a mess."

He smiled tenderly, the happiness strengthening inside

as her eyes lit up with delight. Such a brave little girl. They had to snap the bone back in place. The tears and cries that left her mouth had broken his heart. Lynn had clutched her daughter through it all, while he stood to the side with a hand on Lynn's shoulder. He had felt helpless. Just like all those times his mother had lain in bed with so much pain. He hated that damn hospital. Thank god, they were back at his house.

"What's my mom doing?" She took a small sip. Her eyes closed briefly, her smile never wavering.

She liked it. His mom really was the pro, even his dad could make a mean hot chocolate, but Elliot could only do it so-so.

"Talking on the phone with Ashley's mom. How's the arm feeling, kiddo?"

"It's okay. What happens if the pain comes back? I want to be a big girl for my mom. I don't want to cry again."

Just like that, the ache came back. He scooted closer to her on the couch and softly pulled her into his side. "You don't have to put on a brave front for your mom. I broke my arm once. I cried and cried and cried. You know what my mom did? She held me like I am with you and she didn't care how much I cried. Just like your mom doesn't. You can cry whenever you want."

"I feel like a baby when I cry."

"It's okay to cry. I cry, even at this age."

"Really? What makes you cry?" Laura tilted her head to look at him while her hand clutched the mug with a death-like grip.

Elliot maintained eye contact even though he wanted to look away. "My mom died a few years ago. I couldn't hold in the tears. And it's okay when you can't. Even my dad cried. So, if two big guys like us can cry, you can, too."

Her hand loosened on the mug. "I'm sorry about your mom."

"Me, too, kiddo." He kissed the top of her head and inhaled her sweet innocence. "Just think of all those cool autographs you'll get when you go to school."

"That is pretty neat. Maybe Tim will sign it."

He chuckled, squeezing her lightly. "I bet he'll be the first one."

❄

Lynn wiped a tear from her cheek before stepping into the living room. What a wonderful man to comfort her child. To think Laura thought she had to be brave for her. Never. That was her job.

"How's the hot chocolate? I watched him make it and he wouldn't let me help at all." Elliot started to move, but she waved her hand at him to stay put. She took a seat on the other side of Laura.

"It's awesome! You should have some, Mom."

Lynn tossed an arm around Laura and squeezed lightly. Her hand brushed Elliot's arm. He gazed at her. Just one look relayed how appreciative she was for him making Laura feel better. "I think I might, but we're missing something."

Elliot snapped his fingers. "Marshmallows. How could I forget those?"

"Cookies. You should always have cookies with hot chocolate." Lynn smiled at Elliot as Laura giggled. He thankfully kept his mouth closed that there was a container of cookies still sitting on his counter, but winked mischievously. Making cookies always lifted Laura's spirits.

"We could have marshmallows *and* cookies," Laura said as the light in her eyes brightened.

"Best idea ever. I can't believe I forgot the marshmallows." Elliot shook his head with dismay even as his eyes twinkled with laughter.

"I think we need to teach Elliot how to paint some cookies," Lynn said as she brushed his arm again, truly grateful for his uplifting spirit to make her daughter feel better.

"Oh, don't tease me with cookies. I get some, too, right?" Gregory said as he walked into the living room with Gabby by his side.

Lynn glanced over at them, surprised she didn't hear the front door open. "Only if you help make them."

"Count me in. I've never painted a cookie before. You'll show me, little one?" Gregory asked Laura with a friendly smile.

"That's my dad Gregory, Laura. And standing next to him is…is his girlfriend, Gabby. He'll need a lot of help learning. He's a messy painter," Elliot said with a chuckle as a giggle escaped from Laura.

Lynn stood up and clapped her hands. "Let me get the dough ready. Everyone wash their hands."

Gabby followed Lynn to the kitchen, and with her help, they were quickly ready to start painting the cookies.

"Am I doing it right?" Elliot asked with a grin as he lightly brushed a bright red color onto his sugar cookie while Laura supervised.

Lynn stood for a moment by the counter just appreciating the view. Could he get any sweeter?

"They look awesome, but you gotta be gentle. You'll smoosh the cookies," Laura said, taking a sip of her hot chocolate.

"Cookie's still taste good smooshed, but watch me do it

the right way, Elliot," Gregory said with a wink to Laura, who giggled at his silliness.

"Everyone's doing a wonderful job," Gabby said from behind Gregory. "That hot chocolate looks delicious, Laura."

"Elliot could probably make you some." Laura smiled at her sweetly.

A flash of pain passed through his eyes, so brief, that Lynn was probably the only one to see it before he said, "I can whip up another batch."

"When you're done. No rush, Elliot," Gabby said, then walked over by Lynn. "Your daughter is so sweet. Will your parents be coming for Christmas?"

Lynn's hand stalled on the rolling pin.

"What did I say wrong?"

"I haven't spoken to my parents in over eight years. They were always very strict, very judgmental. It hurts when Laura asks about them. Although, she doesn't ask anymore."

Gabby placed a comforting hand on Lynn's shoulder. "She probably senses that it upsets you. I'm sorry for bringing it up. I had no idea."

"Oh, don't worry about it. I have thick skin."

Lynn glanced over at Elliot again, who was laughing with Laura as she said something funny. She didn't need her parents. She had everything she needed right here in this room. Elliot interacted with her daughter beautifully, almost like a father figure. And Gregory, such a delightful man, treated her like a granddaughter. What would happen if her and Elliot didn't work out?

Elliot laughed again as Laura made a silly face at Gregory and then he joined in on the silly faces. Suddenly, it didn't seem like she had to worry.

"Do you have children?" Lynn asked, turning back to Gabby.

"Two boys and a girl. I lost my dear Phillip and my one son James in a plane crash. Phillip was an excellent flyer, but that day something just went wrong. My other son, Warren, he lives in South Dakota with his family. My daughter, Stacy, she lives in Texas with her family. I wasn't sure which one I planned to see for the holidays, but then Gregory asked me to join him this year."

"I'm so sorry for your loss, Gabby." Lynn wiped her hands on her apron, grabbing a hug from Gabby before she could object.

"What are you two beautiful ladies doing over there? My pan is almost done. I need a refill soon." Gregory laughed as he lifted his pan of cookies.

Gabby pulled away and smiled brightly at Gregory. "Lynn's almost done. Finish that last cookie and I'll give you another pan." He winked at her, making her blush.

Lynn smiled at the interaction, catching Elliot's eye. He had a half-smile, but still a small lingering pain in his eyes as he watched it as well. She blew him a tiny kiss, which made his eyes sparkle with desire. Just like that, she took his pain away.

Lynn turned back toward the counter and added two more cutouts to the pan and handed it to Gabby. She swapped pans with Gregory and tossed the one pan into the oven. Lynn excused herself to use the bathroom as Gabby started to roll more dough.

Lynn took her time using the bathroom. The warm water flowed nicely, soothing her aches for a brief moment. She never wanted to see her baby girl in pain ever again. She leaned closer to the mirror. A hint of dark circles had developed under her eyes. Amazing what a small shock to the system could produce. She looked like she went to hell and back. And she had.

A light knock sounded on the door. She jumped, splashing a small amount of water on her clothes. From behind the door, a soothing voice asked, "You okay, sweetheart?"

Her heart flipped at Elliot's voice and the tender way he called her sweetheart. Something he had recently started to do. Something she didn't want him to stop doing.

She shut the water off, grabbed the towel from the towel rack, and patted her clothes dry. "You can come in."

Elliot slowly opened the door, the concern written in his entire posture. "Everybody seems to be enjoying themselves in the kitchen, but it worried me when you didn't come back." He closed the door and pulled her into his arms. "Is something bothering you?"

She brushed a strand of his hair back that fell onto his forehead. "I was just taking my time. Thank you for everything you've done today. I'm glad you didn't mind the cookie suggestion when I blurted it out. I heard a bit of what Laura said to you. I don't want my baby being brave for me. I'm supposed to be the brave one."

"It was a great idea. Everyone's having fun. She's a tough one. She gets it all from you." He kissed her lips, then wrapped his arms tighter around her. "What I wouldn't do for another sleepover?"

She rested her head against his chest. His warmth and comfort soaked her to the bones. "Me, too. I'm not sure I'm ready to go that level in front of Laura yet."

"I respect any decision you make concerning your daughter. Gabby's almost done rolling out the rest of the dough. Want to help me finish coloring my cookies?"

"I'd love to. For one more kiss." She lifted her head. His eyes twinkled with desire, yet still held concern.

"I think I can handle that."

He dipped his head, claiming her mouth in a fierce kiss. His tongue dove in, tasting, commanding her to tango with him. And she did. Nothing could stop her from keeping pace with him. He caressed his hands down her back, cupping her butt as he pushed her into his hard bulge.

She moaned into his mouth, sinking into his frame as she let the heat swirl around them. She ran her fingers through his hair, pulling on the ends as he pressed her against his erection one more time. The craving to make love to him in the bathroom became so strong that she heaved herself away from his mouth, breathing heavily.

"We should stop, Elliot, before you have me naked against the wall."

He twirled her around, walking her to the wall as he claimed another fiery kiss. "I like you naked against the wall."

She chuckled against his mouth as he tried kissing her yet again. "You make me so happy. I seriously don't understand how I got so lucky to meet you."

Her words had him backing away a step, yet still holding her lightly against the wall. His brows dipped with worry as the light in his eyes dimmed a little. What had she said to make him frown?

"There's nothing to understand. I'm the lucky one. Let's finish those cookies before I start undressing you." He grabbed her hand and led her back to the kitchen.

❄

HOURS LATER, after finishing the cookies, having a light supper, and watching a Christmas movie that they let Laura pick out, Elliot walked back inside the house from waving goodbye to Lynn and Laura.

He joined his dad in the living room, taking a seat next to him on the couch. "Sorry about acting the way I did concerning Gabby."

Gregory glanced at him, happiness reflecting in his eyes. "She's not replacing your mother. Nobody can replace her. Just like I can't replace her late husband, Phillip. Next year, she wants to try and get her family to come home for Christmas. She has three kids, but one passed away with her husband in a plane crash. She'll be joining us this year. That's okay with you, right?"

"That's fine. Lynn really likes her. I had no idea she lost a child and her husband at the same time. That must've been hard."

"I imagine it was, but she's strong. Like your Lynn. And that Laura, she's a hoot. I held my tongue and didn't call her my granddaughter…yet."

Elliot laughed. "Thanks for holding it in." He frowned, rubbing his hands lightly on his thighs. "I think I should tell Lynn that I have her present. That it didn't go to a family in need like it should've. I'm just afraid how she'll react."

"What's the big deal? It brought you together and that's what matters."

"Dad, she's a proud woman. She works hard every day and she probably put a dent in her pocket throwing a twenty in that gift. She still argues with me about paying for her car. I don't think she'd be very happy knowing that I have it and I'm not telling her."

He ran a hand over his face as he blew out a heavy breath. "She keeps saying she can't believe how lucky she is to have met me. Damn it, Dad, it wasn't luck, it was you."

Gregory frowned. "Well, a little bit, but not how you think."

"You set this all up."

Gregory sat up, leaning toward him. "It was all an accident. I stopped at Father Preston's church in Mason to pick up a load of presents for Father Benson. He asked me to drop them off at the firehouse here. You know how the children love seeing the fire truck delivering all the gifts."

"What are you getting at, Dad? Where does Lynn's present come in?"

"I stopped at home, pulled the box of presents out of my car, and dropped the box. Presents went everywhere on the porch. I must've accidentally set that one on the table before I walked inside the house. I didn't stop at the firehouse right away like I planned and I didn't know if leaving the presents out in the cold would be good for them. I didn't want to ruin anything."

Elliot's frown deepened.

"When you came in the house, already having opened the damn present, I just wanted you to feel a little Christmas spirit. I stuck with not knowing where it came from because it made me mad you wanted to give it back. That you couldn't even appreciate a simple gift given to you."

"But it wasn't given to me!"

"Don't holler at me, Elliot." Gregory let out a sigh. "I hate that you don't enjoy the holidays. I thought trying to give it back, you would find the Christmas spirit again. I called Father Preston with a heads up that you'd be there asking questions. You didn't make it to the position of chief of police because you were dumb. He said he'd handle it."

A joyful smile emerged on Gregory's face. "I don't think either of us knew that you and Lynn would fall for each other so deeply. I'm glad I didn't tell you the truth about the present because you've been happier than I've seen you in a long time. You're enjoying the holidays for once because of one woman and her beautiful daughter."

Elliot could do nothing but stare at his dad. Just a bunch of dumb luck landed Lynn in his life. As much as he wanted to be mad at his dad for interfering and keeping secrets, he couldn't. Because Lynn did make him happy.

"Do you really need to tell her? Maybe it was luck and a little faith that had me forgetting it on the porch. Just let it go."

"I can't, Dad. Regardless of how it happened, I need to tell her. I can't have her thinking it was just random luck that I stopped into that diner. It was because a Priest was in cahoots with you. If I'm going to have a relationship that could lead to marriage, I don't want any secrets between us."

"Why do you worry so much?"

Elliot sighed and glanced away.

Gregory snuggled back into his spot, laughing lightly. "You really do worry too much, Elliot. You make it sound like you're holding this intense secret inside of you. I even replaced the gift with a new one, so it's not like a family will be short a gift. Just let it go."

"I'm going to tell her. I have to."

"No matter how you tell her, it'll work out. She loves you."

"I hope so. Because I love her so much it hurts to breathe sometimes."

13

Lynn rushed around the house picking things off the floor, wiping the counters, cleaning the bathroom, and made her bed. Elliot had been to her house the last two days, it's not like he hadn't seen her place a bit messy before. She had no idea how it managed to get so disastrous from the time he left last night to this afternoon. Well, okay, it wasn't that messy. Perhaps she was exaggerating how untidy the house really was. Maybe it was the nerves.

Definitely the nerves. How would Elliot react when she handed over five hundred dollars for her car? She had no idea the total amount it cost to fix her car, since he wouldn't tell her. So she planned to give him what she thought it cost. It was a lot of money. Money that burned a hole in her pocket, and not just because she had so much of it.

No. It was how she managed to get it in the first place.

Would he ask her where she got the money? The bigger question was could she tell him? Thinking about it was making her heart race. What did she do?

Don't think, just clean.

Really, she was panicking for no reason. Elliot, Gregory, and even Gabby, wouldn't care what her house looked like. Tomorrow was Christmas Eve. She had invited everyone to her house for supper, then they all planned to join her and Laura at the church where they would sing carols, like they did every year.

Hopefully the joyous Christmas music would fill her heart back up, diminishing the pain she couldn't seem to clean away.

Or Elliot. She'd let him take the pain away. He could do it. She had faith he would.

Forget the pain. Scrub the tub. Forget the nerves.

Lots of nerves.

She had even been nervous when she invited Elliot over for Christmas Eve. She had no idea why. Their relationship went from simple and new, to complicated and comfortable.

Really, the only complication she could think of was— when would they be able to spend the night together again? Each night Elliot left, she saw the hope and the longing in his eyes to stay with her. But true to his word about respecting her decisions, he left with a smile on his face and a kiss to last her until the next day when she would see him again.

She wanted him to spend the night. She really, really did. She wanted to dive into a full-blown relationship where they talked about moving in together and what the future held. Future, as in, marriage.

But that was crazy even to contemplate. They had known each other almost two weeks. That wasn't very long to know that he was the one.

Would he even want her after she gave him the money? Damn, two complications. So much worse than just having one.

He would understand. If she could manage to tell him the truth, that is. When he finally knew, he would take the pain away and fill it with his love. He had to, or she would fall apart.

Every time he smiled at her with tenderness in his eyes, she swore she saw the love. Every time he helped Laura with her homework, or played a silly game Laura insisted on playing, she saw it again. Just a simple thought of him always made her heart beat rapidly, then plummet to the floor. That was what love felt like to her. Like stepping on a ride that spun her round and round and round, and by the time she had to step off, she'd want to do it all over again because she just couldn't get enough of it.

How could she not love a man that continuously stopped at the diner, grabbing a cup of coffee that he still insisted was delicious, stole a quick kiss from her, and left a tip that shouldn't have been left. A small tip. Small enough where she wouldn't argue with him.

When news spread, and it spread like wildfire, that Lynn Carpenter was dating a man, the diner suddenly had more people than she could keep up with. Everyone in town wanted to know everything about this Elliot they heard about. She smiled politely, gave small non-descript answers to keep them satisfied, and tried not to panic.

She couldn't be mad at anyone for their nosiness because they all left decent tips. Tips she used to buy her remaining presents with. Laura's presents were complete. All bought, wrapped, and tucked away in the closet. She even had enough money to buy Elliot, Gregory, and Gabby a gift.

Of course, she didn't get all that money from tips. Nope. Part of that money came from the deep heartache she created for herself.

A tear slid down. She swiped it away and finished cleaning the bathroom before she let the sadness consume her.

Elliot would be here soon. Her excitement grew just by that thought. Elliot would be coming over tonight, as usual, but the one difference—Laura was having another sleepover at Ashley's house. While Ashley's mother, Tiffany, still felt horrible for what happened on her watch, Lynn had assured her everything would be fine. That she wasn't mad at her. This sleepover, unlike the first one, had been planned for a while. Laura, Ashley, and three other girls in their class had a night of festivities planned.

That was part of the reason Laura had asked to participate in the secret Santa gift exchange last week. Lynn hadn't realized they would be exchanging at the sleepover, but now that she did, she felt better for giving Laura permission to join in on the secret Santa. And they would have fun. Last day of school, and starting out winter break with a sleepover, definitely sounded like fun.

She knew her sleepover would be fun.

Now, all she had to do was finish vacuuming and figure out what to make for supper before Elliot arrived. Tiffany would be picking the girls up from school, so Lynn didn't even need to worry about that. She had already worked her shift at the diner, only a half day, at the insistence of Tara that she should go home. Take a break from all the hard work she had been doing lately was the last thing Tara said before she made her go home.

Or maybe Tara could see the anticipation on Lynn's face to have Elliot all to herself. She didn't argue once. With the extra time off from work, she even stopped at Wacky Wowza's. She had braved the sex aisle all by herself, purchasing a few items that she thought Elliot would enjoy.

She could already see his expression, which instantly sent her body tingling with flames of desire. She needed him here. Now.

Except she still had to wait.

She shut the vacuum off and stood in the middle of the living room.

Pie.

Maybe she'd bake a pie for tomorrow's get-together. She just needed everything to be perfect. Elliot deserved the best. He always treated her that way. She wanted to reciprocate.

Or maybe she just needed something else to take her mind away from the one thing that kept trying to bring her down.

Just the thought of walking into her bedroom to change her clothes would be difficult. Because she knew what would happen. The sadness would consume her once again. Her eyes would zoom to her closet where that faded brown box lay hidden. Full of things that meant the world to her.

Minus one thing.

Her engagement ring Trent bought her on the day he died.

❄

ELLIOT STRAPPED his phone back to his belt and grabbed the bags tighter. He felt like a teenager telling his dad he wouldn't be home tonight. Not that he needed to inform his dad, but just as he would appreciate a call that his dad wouldn't be coming home, Elliot figured he should return the favor.

His dad's chuckling still reverberated in his ears. Why did his dad find it so funny that he was spending the night at Lynn's? Elliot didn't see the humor. The only thing he saw was the image of Lynn wrapped in his arms all night long. The way he wanted it to be every single night. But he couldn't rush her, especially since he hadn't told her about the gift yet. He really should.

His dad had brought it up yesterday morning, wondering why Elliot still felt the need to come clean. He just did. Maybe he was creating it to be a bigger deal than it really was, but he couldn't help it.

He had told his dad to drop it. That he had it all figured out. He would stick with his original plan that popped into his head the other day. He just hoped he wasn't going about this all the wrong way.

His keys jingled in his hand as the worry started to weave its way through his stomach and up to his heart. God, maybe it was a dumb plan. She would run screaming from him. He just knew it. The bags in his other hand started to weigh him down. Should he return everything he just bought? Could he really go through with this?

Cold air swirled around as he blew a breath. Yes, he could. He had to take the chance that Lynn wouldn't run from him.

He unlocked his truck, grabbed for the door handle, and heard the last voice he ever wanted to hear.

"Elliot, good afternoon," Marybeth said sweetly.

He slowly turned toward her, his brows puckered with a frown. "I don't have the time right now, Marybeth. Have a pleasant evening."

She stepped closer to him. Just enough where she could reach out and grab him if she really wanted to. "Elliot, you're not still mad at me, are you? I wasn't lying that night. She did say some really mean things to me. And, quite frankly,

I'm shocked that you believe her over me. You've known me much longer."

"Are you kidding me, Marybeth? Let's just get something straight here. If I wanted to date you, I would've asked you out a long time ago."

She took another step, sliding her body close to his as she wrapped her arms around his neck. "Elliot, let's not pretend. You know you want me. She can't possibly offer you half of what I can. With the looks, with the money, and certainly in the bedroom."

A shiver rushed through from the disgusting feeling of her arms around him. Shit! Did he have time to take a shower before he went to Lynn's?

Never one to cause a scene, he slowly grabbed her hands from around his neck and gently pushed her away. "Have a nice night, Marybeth."

He opened his door. His arm jerked when she clamped a hand around him.

"Why are you lying to yourself, Elliot?"

He turned toward her as he shook her hand off. "Why are you doing this, Marybeth? No means no. I'm sorry to say, *you* can't offer half of what Lynn can. Move on. Find somebody else because it's not happening with me. I never wanted to be mean about it like this, but you're really not giving me a choice."

For the first time, Marybeth's face contorted with real rage.

"I'll tell Lynn you slept with me. That you just took advantage of me right now. I'll tell her so many things that will have you regretting every little thing you just said. You messed with the wrong woman, Elliot." She threw her nose in the air and stalked off across the sidewalk like a woman on a mission.

Elliot climbed into his truck and slammed the door shut.

"Shit!" He banged his hands against the steering wheel. With one deep breath, he pulled his truck out of the parking spot and headed for the one place he had been dying to be all day. Now he dreaded it.

How in the hell did he tell Lynn about this? Would she really believe anything Marybeth spilled from her lips? He sure in the hell hoped not, otherwise he'd be losing Lynn whether he wanted to or not.

※

LYNN SQUEALED with delight as she hung up the phone. Giddy and nervous all in one breath. Elliot was on his way. She ran a hand over her hair, taming down strands that didn't need to be tamed. Deep breath. Why in the world was she acting so crazy? It's not like they hadn't had sex yet. This was nothing new anymore. Like old times.

She laughed. Her smile dimmed as she neared her bedroom. Another deep breath. She could do this.

She walked inside and headed straight for the closet. Her eyes drifted to the left where the box was hidden behind some pillows. She did the right thing. The only thing.

How could she honestly move on with Elliot if she didn't let go of Trent? She would still love him until the end of time, but it was time to make room for a new love. She had obviously started to do that, otherwise she would've never slept with Elliot already. It was time to move on. Seven years in the making.

So why did it feel like her heart was tearing into two?

Think of Elliot. That's the only thing she could do right now. She forced herself to move her gaze away from the top of the closet and looked at her clothes.

More damn nerves. What should she wear? What would he think when he saw all the delicious things she bought? Would he even want to try any of them?

She glanced at the floor of the closet where the Wacky Wowza's bag lay. Maybe she should hide the bag. A small bit of pink fuzz hung out, making the images of Elliot doing naughty things to her bright and clear. Geez, maybe she should take it all out of the bag and scatter it around the bed for him to see.

She started to bend down to pick the bag up and froze. She couldn't do that. Staring at all those things would definitely make her lose her nerve and pack it all up, hiding it in a deep, deep, corner of her closet.

Oh, the irony. She could hide it right next to that faded brown box.

She had never done naughty things with Trent. Picturing doing those things with him wouldn't even come. But Elliot. She could already see the smile that would brighten his face as he eyed all the treasures.

Nope. Can't hide it next to that box.

She grabbed the bag and shoved it behind several pairs of shoes.

Next, she shuffled through her clothes. What to wear? She hadn't expected him to call so soon. He must be just as excited as her.

A black dress pierced her eyes. Her hands glided down the smooth fabric. She never wore this dress. There was a reason she never wore it. It revealed way too much. Too much cleavage, too much leg, too much of her backside.

Perfect. She'd seduce him right when he walked through the door. Supper could wait.

Plus, she was itching to get out of here. That box still

pressed on her mind. Could she even have sex with Elliot without that box dropping into her thoughts? Perhaps she should hand him the money first, then sex.

Much better plan.

She snatched the dress from her closet before she could change her mind. Fifteen minutes later, she was applying a small amount of makeup on when she heard the phone ring. She dropped her eye shadow on the counter and ran to the kitchen.

"Hello," she said with a husky voice.

"Oh, sweetheart, don't talk like that, you'll have me harder than a rock in one second. Damn, like right now," Elliot said with a laugh.

"Sorry, I had to run to the phone. Are you almost here? I have something for you."

"What do you have for me? Something sexy?"

She smiled as the bag of goodies floated before her. "I have the money for fixing my car. Five hundred dollars, to be exact." There. She said it. And damn it, the pain was still there.

There was a moment of silence. "Lynn, I don't want your money. Where did you get that kind of money?"

"It doesn't matter. What matters is I have the money to pay you back." Oh, why did she tell him over the phone?

"I don't want your damn money, Lynn."

She jerked as if he slapped her. "What's wrong, Elliot? You never talk like that to me."

He sighed heavily. "I can't come right now. I got a call. As soon as I'm done taking care of this problem, I'll be over. I'm really sorry. I didn't mean to snap, but I'm not taking a dime from you."

Her heart plummeted to the floor. Did he really have to go somewhere? Or did the mention of paying him back make him create a problem that he needed to respond to? "Okay. I know how your job is. Take your time. We have all night."

"And I plan on using the entire night. You won't be getting any sleep."

Pretend like everything was okay. Just pretend. "Promise?"

He chuckled, although, the happiness didn't come through. "That's one promise I will keep."

She hung up the phone and walked back to the bathroom. What just happened?

She probably just seriously screwed up one of the best things to walk into her life.

Stop!

He'd said he had to take care of something and he'd be over. It's not like his job never pulled him away before. Nothing to worry about.

Except maybe the part where they argued about money again when he finally got here.

One thing at time. Finishing her makeup would be a good place to start. She took her time applying her eye shadow, a small dose of blush, and lipstick. She debated mascara, but she really hated putting that crap on. She always managed to miss an eyelash, smearing a chunk on her face every single time. It's not like Elliot would care either way. Not when he saw her in this dress.

Or would he?

No more negative thoughts. He'd love this dress. She couldn't believe the thing still fit. She bought it three years ago on the whim. She had seen it on the rack, feeling depressed that she hadn't been on a date in forever and purchased it to cheer herself up. Maybe bring a bit of good luck on the dating front. She was asked out three weeks later, but lost the nerve to actually wear it on the date. Thank goodness, too, because it would've been wasted on a guy who couldn't stop talking about himself. He couldn't have been more conceited if he tried.

Two hours later, she was slumped on the couch waiting for Elliot to call. He'd be here sooner or later. She just preferred sooner rather than later. She had never been a clingy girlfriend, or even dated enough to be considered someone's girlfriend, at least since Trent passed away.

But the temptation to call him had her tossing the phone back and forth in her hands. She kept the tossing up to stop herself from following through on the action of dialing. She wouldn't bother him. He was busy. She didn't want to disturb him and make, whatever the situation was, worse.

She jumped up from the couch, nearly tripping over her feet when she heard a knock on her door. Deep breaths. They would not fight. She wouldn't let it get to that.

He had decided to surprise her. She sat waiting, worried, and on edge for him to get here, but he was here and that's all that mattered.

She opened the door with a smile. It fell instantly into a frown.

"What are you doing here?" Lynn asked Marybeth, who looked like her normal glamorous self. "And how in the world did you find out where I live?"

"Elliot told me." Marybeth's sweet smile grew into a smirk that had Lynn's skin crawling with unease. "Were you waiting for him? It certainly looks like it."

"What do you want?"

"I'm just trying to help you see what sort of man he is. I told you he was leading you on. You look very pretty, but I'm not sure he'll fall head over heels when he just had this."

Marybeth untied her belt and opened her coat for Lynn to take a good look.

She wore a red dress that accentuated all of her curves. While Lynn never thought of herself as having a small chest, looking at Marybeth's breasts stick out with brilliance, made her realize how much she lacked in that department. No tiny pouch stuck out on her stomach like the one Lynn had. Baby fat she just couldn't get rid of. And her legs, tan, shiny, and looking smooth to the touch. Lynn hated to think that Marybeth did look better.

Wait, what? This was exactly what Marybeth wanted her to think. Elliot would never lead her on. He would never sleep with her one night and jump into bed with another woman the next. She refused to fall into this obvious trap. "Is there any other reason for this visit? I really have nothing to say to you."

"Are you sure? Don't you want to know what we just did? We exerted a lot of energy in the bedroom. He might not have much energy left for you. I'm terribly sorry to tell you that."

"You're lying." Lynn refused to believe any word she just said.

"I'm not. Ask him yourself. Or better yet, wait for him to bring me up. He'll deny it because he wants to string you along a little bit more. He wants me. I'm trying to help you see that."

"I don't believe you." She wouldn't believe anything this woman said, yet she heard the doubt in her own voice. So did Marybeth.

She laughed softly and took a few steps toward her car. "You do believe me." She looked back at Lynn with a quizzical look. "Why isn't he here yet? He left his office forever ago."

Lynn slammed the door. She wouldn't let Marybeth get into her head. She didn't believe her. She was lying, just like she had the night of the Christmas party.

Then, the phone call from Elliot earlier punched her in the gut. He didn't specifically say what he had to do. She just assumed it had to do with work. He wouldn't really delay coming over to her house to spend time with Marybeth, would he? He defended her at the party. She couldn't believe he would sleep with that woman.

Had the argument over money sent him into that woman's arms? Did she do this to herself? He had snapped at her. Something he had never done before.

She shifted that phone call over and over in her mind. He had been slightly angry and then there had been worry. What would he be worried about? Her finding out that he was lying. That he was making his way to Marybeth's instead.

No!

She didn't believe that woman. She was a liar. Marybeth just wanted to hurt her in any way possible because Elliot didn't want her.

She tried to comfort herself with those words until she couldn't take it any longer. She grabbed the phone and dialed his number. She swore loudly when he didn't pick up. Why wasn't he answering?

His house phone. Maybe he went home. She almost sighed in relief when Gregory answered, but too much anxiety kept her from relaxing as she paced back and forth.

"Hi, Gregory. I was looking for Elliot. He didn't answer his cell and…and I just wanted to make sure he was alright. He called me earlier saying he had to take care of a problem and, well, he hasn't called yet. I'm being silly. You know, never mind. Sorry for calling."

"Don't hang up the phone, Lynn," Gregory said with urgency. "I was just going to call you."

Her legs gave out as she slumped onto the couch. "You were? Why's that?"

"It's about Elliot. You're not going to want to hear this. It has me shaken to the bone right now."

The strain in his voice crushed her heart.

Marybeth. She hadn't been lying.

And Gregory knew.

"I can't hear it, Gregory. Don't tell me. I already know."

She hung up before he could say another word.

14

The phone echoed throughout the house. Why did Gregory insist on making it worse? She didn't need to hear the betrayal from him as well. Once was enough from Marybeth.

When it started to ring again after her first refusal to answer, she couldn't take it anymore. Not to mention, it wasn't Gregory's fault. He didn't do anything wrong.

"Please, Gregory, I understand. You don't have to tell me."

"Don't you dare hang up on me again, young lady," Gregory said sternly as if he were her father and he could speak to her in such a way.

Oddly enough, Lynn enjoyed the way he spoke. It told her he cared. She tried to keep the tears at bay, sniffling her nose to stop the torrential downpour. "I'm sorry."

"I just got the call. I guess Elliot must've told them to call you as well."

His heavy breathing, the worry in his tone, confused her. Were they talking about the same thing? "What are you talking about? Isn't this about Marybeth?"

"No, why would you think that?" He sighed heavily. "I don't know what made you think that, but we'll talk about it later. Elliot's been shot. He's—"

"Don't say that!" Lynn stood up, interrupting him before he could say any more horrible words. "Oh, Gregory, if you say he died, I'll...please don't say that."

The torture she put herself through earlier. Taking the brown faded box down from the closet. Opening and closing it several times before she had the nerve to leave the lid open. Pulling out the engagement ring. Keeping it out of the box without shedding a tear. The drive to the store to sell it. And actually handing it over to the salesman. They had played tug of war before she finally let the ring go.

She had let it go. She sold the ring Trent had given her and let go a part of his love. For Elliot. Not just for the money. But to let him in her heart. Now Gregory had to say the most horrible words to her. He couldn't be dead.

"Calm down, Lynn. Please, my heart can't take this. They said it wasn't bad, but I don't know much yet. He's at Mulberry Hospital. I'll come pick you up."

Relief quickly zapped her straight to the soul. He wasn't dead. She could survive as long as he hadn't died.

"I'll meet you there."

"Lynn, honey, you're in hysterics. You can't drive. I won't have the possibility of you getting hurt on my conscience. I'm coming to get you."

She inhaled a deep breath and let it out slowly. She had to stay strong and in control. Sound confident when she wasn't anything close to that. "He's your son. You should be there right away. I'll meet you at the hospital and that's final, Gregory."

He gave in. Lynn hung up the phone before he could object any further. She ran to her room, her heart beating double time where she thought it would never come down from its high. She felt like she was on that ride again, except this time it wouldn't stop. It wouldn't let her off to catch her breath. She needed it to stop. She needed all of her wits about her to drive safely. Gregory was right. Damn near hysterical. The panic coursed through each and every bone. The shakes consumed her. Her nerves were stretched to the limit. Elliot had to be okay.

Not once did her eyes or mind travel to the brown faded box hidden on the top shelf of her closet. Only Elliot's handsome face penetrated her frazzled mind.

She grabbed the hem of her dress and yanked up a little too roughly. Her fingernail hooked the top layer of her skin, the pain almost unbearable as she started to lose her balance and hop on her foot. She landed hard on her butt, the dress halfway off and almost covering her eyes.

The air felt thick with disgrace as she sat there frozen. Absolutely ridiculous. That's what she looked like. Dress halfway off. Dignity lost when she fell.

Elliot needed her. So did Gregory. She had to calm down.

She slowly finished taking the dress off and tossed it near her closet, unconcerned about putting it into the hamper or hanging it back up.

Dignity slightly more intact, she stood up and rubbed her butt. "Gregory shouldn't worry about me getting in a car crash and hurting myself. I seem to be doing a lovely job inside the house."

She lifted her right leg to the bed and inspected her cut. A long red scratch, deeper than she imagined, ran a few inches from her knee to the top of her thigh. Damn nail. Cutting her nails would have to go on her to-do list. Utterly ridiculous.

She grabbed a pair of jeans and shirt from the closet and dressed quickly, but very carefully. She snatched her purse and keys from the kitchen, and all but ran to her car. Her feet did a slippery tango, almost losing her balance as some snow still lingered on the ground. More like a homemade ice pond right on her driveway.

She flopped into her seat and released several breaths before jamming the key into the ignition. "Drive slow, Lynn. You can't be there for Elliot if you get into another crash."

Her little pep talk did the trick. She made it to the hospital twenty-five minutes later, after following every speed limit sign she saw. She knew if she went even a mile over the limit she would've pressed the pedal to the floor without a thought or care in the world. It had been safer for everyone, including herself, that she took it slow and easy, even as her heart pounded rapidly with a twirling dizziness.

As soon as she exited her car, she went from running like a maniac to slowing her steps down to a waddle as she made her way into the hospital. If anyone saw her, they probably wondered if she was heading to the mental ward. That's exactly how she felt. Way too many turbulent emotions to walk steady.

Erin, the wonderful nurse who always seemed to be working whenever Lynn showed up at this dreadful place, was sitting behind the counter as she entered.

"Where is he? How bad is it? Is it—"

Erin rushed around the counter, grabbing Lynn's arm in a comforting embrace. Something she had desperately needed. "Lynn, calm down. He's fine. It's really not that bad."

Erin led Lynn into exam room 10 where Elliot sat on the bed with Gregory next to him. The minute Lynn saw him not hooked to tubes and a small smile on his face, she almost collapsed to the floor. If not for Erin standing next to her, grabbing a hold of her arm again, she would have.

"Lynn." Elliot started to get out of the bed.

"No!" Lynn smiled appreciatively at Erin and rushed over to Elliot. "You need to stay in bed. You've been shot."

She scanned him from head to toe. He still wore his nice gray slacks, but with a blue scrub for a shirt. "Where were you shot?"

Elliot grinned, took her hand, and guided her to sit next to him. "I wasn't shot. A bullet grazed me. The extent of my injury was blown a little out of proportion."

"Grazed? I think that still counts as getting shot." Her brows dipped as she took him all in again.

"I agree," Gregory added.

"I'm fine. I don't know why Officer Johnson called you and told you the way he did, Dad." Elliot kissed Lynn's hand, obviously trying to calm her down. It barely worked. "I'm fine, sweetheart. I promise."

"You didn't call me, Elliot." Keeping the accusatory tone out of her voice was impossible. Although, with Gregory in the room, she should've controlled it better.

He winced. "I busted my phone in the process. I would never intentionally ignore you about something like this."

"Where are you hurt?" she asked, still trying to figure out where he was *grazed*, as he put it. Not to mention, having an argument in front of Gregory wasn't ideal. She sensed one brewing in the air. Her fault, of course, for attacking him like that with her sharp tone.

"My shoulder. It's not that bad." He started to lift his arm to show her he barely felt it, except he winced in pain, not able to lift it any farther. "Dr. Pearson had to stitch me up a little. But really, it's just a graze."

"Stitches do not constitute, 'just a graze,' Elliot." Did he think this was funny? He could've been seriously hurt.

Gregory must've sensed the growing tension. He pulled his phone out of his pocket and grinned. "I'm going to call Gabby. I'll be right back."

As soon as he left the room, Elliot pulled Lynn closer, kissing her with intense passion. A passion that calmed her down a tiny bit from the fear that had gutted her. He tugged on her bottom lip. "I'm sorry if I scared you. My dad said he was worried about you driving here. I was worried myself until you walked in."

She brushed her lips against his, savoring his intoxicating taste. Just a little bit more reassurance that he was safe. "It was a bit of a shock. One right after the other."

He leaned back, his one hand still holding hers. He reached up with his sore arm, wincing, yet gently caressed her cheek. "You're talking about Marybeth? My dad told me what you said. What happened? Whatever she said, it's a lie."

She took his hand that still held her cheek and slowly brought it down to her lap. Instant relief hit his eyes. Yet, she knew he still would've comforted her in any way he could. That's just the sweet man he was. "She came to my home."

"How in the hell did she know where you live?"

"She said you told her."

He grabbed her hand harder. "I would never tell her that. Never. Do you believe me?"

The pain wasn't just in her hand from his fierce grip, but also in his eyes. "She said some interesting things. I had a moment of panic and needed to hear your voice. You didn't answer your cell, so I tried the house phone. Then Gregory said he had to tell me something and her words rang true for a moment. I had no idea it was something like this."

The torture increased in his expression as he puckered his eyebrows. "Lynn, you ignored my question. You don't believe me."

"I believe you."

"Then give me a smile."

There wasn't much to smile about when they talked about that woman. But he was okay. She could smile about that. She produced a small smile for his benefit.

His deep frown remained. "What else did she say?"

"It doesn't matter."

"It does. I want to know. No matter what she said, it's not true. She stopped me in town today. I turned her advances down and she didn't like that. She told me that she would tell you we slept together. But I would never do that. Please believe me, Lynn."

"I do. I even told her I didn't believe her."

He gripped her hand again. "Why does it sound like you do believe her?"

She leaned in and kissed him. "You scared the living daylights out of me, Elliot. You were shot. Forgive me if I'm having a hard time getting past that."

His frown slowly died as a sexy grin formed. "So we're still on for tonight?"

"I'd like that."

"We need to leave. I need you now," he whispered as he pulled her closer and nibbled on her bottom lip.

"You're hurt."

"It's a graze. It's not going to stop me from having you under me tonight."

"Elliot, don't say things like that so loud." She laughed as he wiggled his eyebrows in playful delight. "I am really starting to hate this hospital. I don't ever want to see it again."

"I agree. It's much easier when you're by my side, though."

"You didn't tell me how this happened. Who shot you?" She brushed a hand across his cheek as the sadness came back into his eyes.

"Grazed, remember." His smiled died as the next words left his mouth. "Fred showed up at his wife's house, even after the judge ordered him to stay away when he was released on bail for assaulting Stu. The judge felt like he was a danger, not just to Stu, but to his wife as well. He was right. I went there to defuse the situation. I didn't know he had a gun. I don't think he meant to fire it, but it went off before I even knew he had the thing. Luckily, he missed."

Lynn hovered her hand over his injured shoulder. "He didn't miss."

"You know what I mean. I dropped to the ground to dodge any more bullets, pulling my weapon out at the same time. That's how I busted my phone. Before I could even point my gun at him, he was on the ground crying, weeping like a baby how sorry he was."

Elliot sighed heavily, moving his shoulder a little and winced. "I think I'm done trying to help my friend out of these situations. I told my officers to quit calling me and just do their job from now on concerning him. He shot the chief of police, so I don't think he's going to get a nice bail from the judge this time."

"Shot you, huh? I thought it was a graze." She smirked at him playfully, receiving a small chuckle from him.

"I have serious plans for you tonight."

She cupped his face and kissed him, expressing everything in that simple kiss what she wanted to do tonight. "You might not be getting everything you want tonight. You're hurt."

"I'll get down on my knees and beg if I have to. I want you, Lynn, and I'm having you."

She smiled tenderly as she stood up from the bed. "I'll go find Dr. Pearson about discharging you. It's too bad about the stuff I bought."

"What did you buy?"

She walked toward the door, glancing at him with desire in her eyes. "I stopped at Wacky Wowza's. I ventured into a certain aisle, picking out a few things I thought you'd like."

He sat up in bed, shifting a little. The desire spiked in every facet of his body. "And just why is it too bad you bought this stuff? Tell me what you bought."

"You're hurt, Elliot. Some of the stuff requires certain movements and you can't move your shoulder without wincing. I guess I'll save it for another day. Or maybe even return it all." She sighed heavily, turning toward the door as she tried to hold in her laughter.

Laughter felt good. She was starting to develop the same aversion to hospitals as Elliot. She couldn't stand the sight of him in that bed.

"You're not returning anything, sweetheart. Get over here. I want to know what you bought. Screw Dr. Pearson, we're leaving now."

She looked over her shoulder at him, unable to stop the laugh from escaping. "Now, now, Elliot, you'll wait for me to find Dr. Pearson."

"I'm not waiting. You're in for it when we get to your house." He adjusted his position again.

"You promise?"

"Damn right, I promise."

This time his promise rang with truth and sincerity.

※

TWO HOURS LATER, after filling his prescription, visiting with Gabby, who came the minute Gregory told her what happened, and receiving the discharge papers from Dr. Pearson, Elliot and Lynn made it to Mason.

The minute they walked into her house, Elliot tried to veer Lynn to her bedroom, but she insisted he eat first. He reluctantly let her play mother as she fed him, made sure he was comfortable as he ate, and practically shoved a pain pill down his throat as she obviously continued to notice him wince in pain.

For some reason, he saw pain in her eyes. He didn't think it had anything to do with his injury.

"What's the matter, Lynn?"

She stopped grabbing for his empty plate from the table and glanced away. "We need to talk."

Words a man never wanted to hear.

He snatched her hand before she could actually grab the plate and pulled her into his lap. She gasped with surprise, giving him the perfect opportunity to dig in with a deep kiss. She hesitated for a moment, then wrapped her arms around his neck and hung on for the ride. He savored her sweet taste for a long time before gently nipping her bottom lip and drew her away. Just a few inches from his lips in case he needed to kiss her words away again.

"What's wrong?"

"I have your money for fixing my car. I want to give it to you."

"I don't want your money."

She started to open her mouth to protest. He dove in again, kissing away her words. She trailed her hands up into his hair, weaving her fingers through his thick locks. Then, surprisingly, she grabbed tightly and yanked his mouth away. He winced from the slight pain.

"You can't keep distracting me with a kiss every time we talk about money."

"Why? There's nothing to talk about. I don't want your money. Consider it a Christmas gift."

His hands tightened on her waist when it felt like she wanted to get up.

"It's not just about the money, Elliot."

He wiped a tear as it slid down her cheek. "What did I do? What are you saying, Lynn?"

"You asked earlier how I got that much money."

"I am curious."

She hung her head down. He wouldn't let her pull away from him like that. He grabbed her chin and lifted. Her beautiful brown eyes shimmered with so much pain. "Fine. I'll take the money. I hate arguing with you. Just don't say I'm losing you, Lynn. I don't want to hear that."

"Don't you want to know how I got that much money?"

"Short of robbing a bank, it doesn't matter. When you want to tell me, you will."

"You seem too good to be true sometimes."

He scooped her body close to his chest and stood up. "I just want to make you happy."

"You have no idea how much you do."

He started for the bedroom. "I can't wait anymore."

She rested her head against his chest, then must've realized what he was doing. "Put me down, Elliot. Your shoulder."

"It's fine." Besides the small shooting pains converging down his arm. Completely fine. He'd be damned if he put her down.

"You've never lied before, Elliot, don't start now."

He sheepishly smiled as he set her down on the bed.

"Okay, it hurts a little. But not enough to keep me from loving you. Where are the things you bought me?"

He didn't give her time to interpret his words about love. He had meant them more than just loving her between the sheets. After the near scare she gave him out in the dining room, he needed to show her just how much he loved her. She hadn't exactly reassured him everything was okay. She was holding something back from him. Something she deemed important.

But that was okay. He was holding something back from her. That damn present.

She giggled. "We'll save that for when you are up to full power."

"I'm not a patient man. I want it now."

"Tough, mister. My house, my rules."

"I'll remember that." His smile said that she would be in for it the next time she spent the night at his house.

"Fair enough." She pushed him back to let her stand up. "Let me help you get undressed."

"By all means. I like this pampering."

"Well, that doesn't mean you can get hurt like this again just so I'll pamper you."

"Sweetheart, I swear I'll try never to get shot—grazed again in my life. Trust me."

The slip-up of his words had her gathering him in her arms and resting her head against his chest. "I was really scared tonight when your dad said you were shot. I can't lose you...especially like that."

"You'll never lose me." He kissed the top of her head, then bit his lip. He couldn't profess his love yet. He had to stick to his plan.

"Hey, you're supposed to be undressing me," he whispered into her ear, taking a nibble, then chuckled as she moaned at the touch.

He started to place small, light kisses from her ear down her neck before she finally pushed him back. "I lead this time. No touching."

"No promises there, sweetheart. I can't help myself."

He kept his hands to himself as she helped take his shirt off. When she pulled down his jeans and started to reach for his boxers, he couldn't contain his control. He reached out for her, but she moved out of the way laughing.

"Nope. No touching." She pointed to the bed.

He cocked his lips in a devious grin, debating whether to listen. Her saucy smile had him climbing on the bed with delightful anticipation. Damn, what a gorgeous woman!

He rested against the pillow, only finding true comfort when she started to slowly take off her shirt and pants. She did a little dance, moving her body to a sensual tune as she unhooked her bra and slid her panties down. She crawled onto the bed like a predator looking at her prey, then removed his boxers with slow precision.

"I can't take much more," he groaned roughly.

❄

"Shh, let me take care of you." She started at his mouth, kissing him lightly. She laughed a little when he growled at her departure.

She carefully placed kisses on his chest, taking her time to cover every curve and groove. The smooth feeling of his body, the hard ridges, the sprinkles of chest hair that made a nice little trail to the heat she craved drove her wild with need. So brazen. She never acted like this.

She followed the trail like a pirate looking for treasure.

When she finally made contact with her prize, he lifted up slightly and groaned with desire. She took him fully into her mouth, playing, teasing. Her desire spiked every time he moved with her.

"Shit, Lynn. You have to stop. I need you," he whispered roughly, brushing his hands in her hair.

Ignoring every word, she continued to build his desire to a burning need. She had never done anything of this sort on any man. Not even Trent. The power she had over him, urged her to take him deeper as he kept pace. Her path of kisses paled in comparison to this. She knew it without even asking. He told her with every movement, every groan, every small tug on her hair.

"Please, Lynn, I'm so close, but I want to be inside you," he murmured in between heavy breaths.

Suddenly, she needed that as well. She sucked hard on his tip before releasing him completely. "Did you like that?"

"Don't ask silly questions, sweetheart. My turn." He started to sit up when she put a hand on his chest.

"Nope." Another gentle push and he laid back down. She reached over to her nightstand and pulled a condom out.

Every time a tiny groan left his mouth, she couldn't help but tease him. Sheathing him became a slow torture that mirrored in his eyes whenever he glanced at her. God, she loved that sound he made. That yearning look he gave her.

Before he could do anything, like flip her onto her back and take over, she cradled her body over the top of him and gently slid down onto his hard erection.

"Much better." He smiled as he pulled her closer to his lips.

The kiss deepened as she started to move with him. But this was her show. She slid her tongue out, tugging on his lips before sitting back up. Her body rocked to each movement he made, riding him like a cowboy would ride a bull. Every tingle that hit her body zapped her energy to a faster pace. This control, the one who made the decisions on how she would move next, acted like an aphrodisiac.

When the tingles started to increase into zings, she increased the pace further, until the zings turned into explosions. He shuddered beneath her as she rode the waves of ecstasy. She collapsed onto his chest when her body shifted into jelly and she couldn't hold herself up anymore.

He kissed her cheek, breathing deeply. "I like you on top. I loved watching you move like that, your face so full of delight. You're so damn beautiful."

"I have to say, I liked it, too." No energy was left anywhere in her body. Not even to lift her head and kiss him soundly on the lips.

"My turn now," he whispered.

"You're hurt."

"I told you I'd keep you up all night, and that's what I'm going to do. Your touch healed me. It was perfect."

He hit the mark with that one.

Perfect.

And it was. All so perfect. Except for the part where her eyes suddenly shifted to the closet. Why didn't she tell him? His loving touch erased Trent from her mind while they were in the moment. But lying like this, he drifted right back in like gentle waves on a beach. She wouldn't be completely free to love Elliot until she told him.

Soon. If she didn't chicken out again.

15

Elliot slid into the booth, his face expressionless as he eyed Councilman Jerome Jenkins across from him.

"It's Christmas Eve, Chief, and we're meeting at a diner in Mason. Why? I'd like to be at home with my family," Jerome said with a slice of irritation.

"Me, too, Councilman. You know what else I'd like? I would like for your daughter Marybeth to leave me and my girlfriend alone. Normally I would never come to you about something like this, but Marybeth crossed the line."

Before Jerome could respond, the waitress approached their booth. Elliot smiled at Tara as she glanced between the two with a friendly smile. "Good morning, Tara. I'll have a cup of that delicious coffee of yours, and so will my friend."

"Good morning, Elliot. How's Lynn? She told me she's having you and your father over today."

"She's bustling around the kitchen getting everything prepared. She wants everything to be perfect, even though it will be with little effort on her part," Elliot said with a sincere smile.

"I've never seen her happier. And you're right, she works herself to the bone too much. Two coffees, coming right up." Tara smiled brightly, although, eyed Jerome with a leery look before she walked away.

Elliot closed his lips tightly to keep the laughter in. Tara obviously had a good sense of people, and she sensed Jerome as a possible threat.

"So, please, tell me what my daughter could have possibly done. Acting a little childish, aren't we, Chief?" Jerome leaned back, folding his hands on the table, the irritation becoming stronger.

"I've tried to be polite. I've tried to tell her nicely that whatever she thinks there is between us, there isn't. She tried to accuse Lynn of assaulting her. It's against the law to report a crime that didn't actually happen."

"I know the law," Jerome grounded out as he pursed his lips.

Elliot cleared his throat, offering Tara a smile as she came back to their table with two steaming cups of coffee. "Thank you so much, Tara. And merry Christmas."

"You're very welcome, Elliot. And merry Christmas. You tell Lynn, and that beautiful daughter of hers, that I said it as well." Tara gave a guarded smile to Jerome as she walked away.

Elliot looked back at Jerome, who still had his lips pressed together, the impatience buzzing around. Enough of this. So he didn't like what he had to say about his daughter. Well, tough. The truth hurt sometimes.

"Yesterday she threatened to ruin my relationship with Lynn by spreading lies. Who is the child?"

Elliot took a sip of coffee. He knew Jerome wouldn't say another thing until he finished everything he had to say.

"She showed up at Lynn's house, unannounced. I'd like

to know where she got that information. If I really want to dig and find out, I could. But I won't if she leaves us alone. Here's the deal, Councilman. You make sure that your daughter never bothers me or Lynn again. Because if she does, I'll be helping Lynn to file a restraining order for harassment. I will even go as far as meeting with Chief Brown here in Mason and file harassment charges. We both know the fallout of either of those things happening wouldn't look good on Marybeth...or you."

Elliot gripped his coffee cup harder. "We've always been friendly, cordial, and I've always respected you. That's why I'm coming to you, as a courtesy. I know trying to talk to Marybeth that she won't listen to anything I have to say."

"She's always been someone who wants what she wants," Jerome said flippantly.

"Yeah, well, she's not getting her way this time. I know what I want, and that's Lynn."

"She won't bother either of you again. I'll talk to her." Jerome finally took a drink from the cup in front of him. "It's too bad you don't see her differently. Our families have always been close."

Elliot tried not to roll his eyes or shift in his seat like a million disgusting bugs were crawling everywhere. Talk about a nightmare if that ever happened. And Jerome was a prejudice man. He normally didn't approve of the men Marybeth always eyed with delight. Elliot had also heard a few rumors that Jerome muttered a few irritations when Elliot nabbed the chief of police position. Jerome may be friends with his father, but that didn't mean Jerome liked him. Very strange he would want him dating his daughter.

Unless Jerome thought he'd have more control over him if he married Marybeth. Damn! Was everything that happened because of Marybeth or her father? She always did what the man told her to.

Nothing he'd worry about now. He'd make both their lives hell if they didn't leave him and Lynn alone.

Jerome stood up, pulled out his wallet and threw a twenty on the table. "I think we're done here." He grabbed his jacket from the seat, sliding it on with ease. "Merry Christmas, Chief. Don't call me again."

"Merry Christmas. I don't plan on it." Elliot took another drink of his coffee as Jerome walked away.

A large breath escaped as he took another sip of coffee. Dreadful conversation completed. He couldn't say he disliked Jerome, but he also wasn't his favorite person. He could be condescending with no remorse whatsoever. He could also be your best friend—when he really wanted something. He had tried to sway Elliot many times into doing things a certain way. Elliot listened like he cared, but did his job the way he wanted to.

Yeah, it wasn't so far off to think Jerome wanted Marybeth to get him in her clutches. He definitely dodged a bullet there.

Elliot finished his coffee, threw another twenty next to Jerome's, waved a quick goodbye to Tara, and headed to his truck.

When he walked back into Lynn's house, he found her in the kitchen. He leaned against the wall, watching as she swayed back and forth in front of the stove while she listened to Christmas music. This would never get old. She looked happy, carefree, and the most beautiful woman he had ever met, even covered in the stains she created on her apron from all the baking and cooking she had been doing the entire morning.

Lynn turned around, screaming a little when she saw

him staring at her. "You shouldn't surprise me like that. Or look at me like that."

He stood up, taking a step into the kitchen. "Like what?"

She backed up with a sweet smile. "Like you want to devour me."

"Maybe I do." He snagged a hand around her waist before she could escape him. Then he kissed her. "You're working too hard. Why don't you take a break?"

"Perhaps you should rest. You were shot yesterday."

He nuzzled her neck, inhaling the smell of cinnamon that lingered on her. "We talked about this. Grazed, not shot."

"How did it go? What took you so long?"

"I think Marybeth's smart enough to listen to her father." No need to tell her about his suspicions about the real reason Marybeth acted the way she had. Lynn didn't need any more worry in her life.

Because she was still worrying about something. She handed him five hundred dollars this morning without one argument from him. He refused to see her cry again. Those tears last night had been his fault. He certainly didn't want her to force out of him what her car really cost. It hadn't been anywhere near five hundred dollars. His little secret he didn't mind keeping. He did, however, want to know the secret she seemed to be hiding.

"I stopped at the store afterwards."

"For what?"

He kissed her again, taking his time to savor her sweet lips. She tasted like chocolate. He knew why, too. She kept a bag of chocolate next to her as she worked, popping a piece in every so often. She told him, when he asked right before he left, that it helped her concentrate while she baked. He couldn't help but smile when she said that. He took a nibble of her lip before he pulled away.

"Not telling. It's a surprise. Sort of how you wouldn't tell me last night what you bought from a certain aisle." He winked at her as he let her go and walked toward the fridge.

"You stopped at Wacky Wowza's and bought...things?" Lynn asked as her eyes frantically looked at the doorway as if Laura was about to magically appear.

He pulled a bottle of water out of the fridge and walked over to the counter where his prescription sat. "I'm not telling. You'll have to wait and see."

"Fine." She turned around to the stove. "Leave the kitchen so I can have everything ready before your dad and Gabby arrive."

"I wish you'd take a break with me. You really are working too hard. Let's play a game with Laura."

He walked over by the stove, wrapping his arms around her from behind. He lowered his lips to her ear, kissing, nibbling, and teasing her. "Please take a break."

"I'm trying to make some gravy for the mashed potatoes." She moved her head to the side to give him better access.

Oh, to have the house alone again. The things he would do to her right here in the kitchen.

"The gravy can wait. Laura and I can't." He trailed a few kisses down her neck, then slowly peppered soft kisses back to her ear. "Laura wanted me to teach her some card games when I got back. Play with us."

She released a soft moan when he rubbed a hand over her breast, caressing her nipple with teasing delight. "You better stop, Elliot. If Laura walks in..."

"She'll see me holding you, helping to stir the gravy," he whispered. He kissed her neck one more time before stepping away. He grabbed her hand and turned the burner off. "You'll have fun, I promise."

"I'm sure I will. You have yet to disappoint me."

"And I hope I never do."

Except about the present. Disappointment could very well swoop in and have her shoving the door in his face.

※

Lynn waited on the top step of the church as Elliot and Father Preston talked inside the building. What could they possibly be talking about? He had excused himself when he saw Father Preston, rushing over to him with an expression she couldn't decipher. They immediately started smiling, talking, and laughing like old friends. She had no idea Elliot knew him.

Gregory and Gabby were waiting at the bottom of the steps. They were both very active in their church. Perhaps that's how Elliot knew Father Preston. She knew that Mason and Mulberry interacted quite frequently on events within each town. Or maybe his position as chief of police had him knowing quite a few people that she normally wouldn't know.

A puzzle. One that slightly bugged her. Why did it bug her? Who knew. But when Elliot finally joined them a few minutes later, she smiled as if nothing had been on her mind. And there wasn't. Not when he grabbed her hand as natural as could be, planted a sweet kiss on her lips, and tossed a tender arm around Laura.

"Let's go, my beautiful ladies," Elliot said as they started down the steps.

"That was wonderful. I haven't sung like that in ages,"

Gabby said, as they finally joined them. "It's such a lovely church."

"And you have a wonderful voice, my dear." Gregory kissed her cheek, then looked at Lynn. "Thank you so much for the delicious meal, Lynn. You outdid yourself. I'm not sure our meal will be as good tomorrow."

"It'll be great, I'm sure. What time should Laura and I come tomorrow?" Lynn asked, looking at Gregory, even though she stood next to Elliot holding his hand.

Why didn't she ask him? The day had been great with not one argument between them, but she still hadn't told him about the ring even when she handed him the money. That would've been the ideal time to tell him. Such a chicken!

"You're welcome anytime. I'm sure Elliot would like to spend the day with you. We can have lunch ready, not just supper." Gregory rested his head against Gabby's. "This one will be joining us for both. She wants to make lasagna for lunch. A special recipe, according to her."

"You'll love it. My kids devour it the minute it touches their plates." Gabby laughed when Gregory whispered something in her ear, slapping his arm playfully.

"Anytime you guys want to come is fine with me." Elliot looked at Lynn and Laura, the hope clearly written in his eyes they came as early as possible.

"Aren't you spending the night, Elliot?" Laura asked, her eyes wide with eagerness.

"Umm...well...I..."

Lynn stifled a laugh at his discomfort. He was always so adorable tongue-tied.

"Because you'll miss Santa if you're not with us. Mom, he can't miss Santa." Laura tugged on Lynn's hand, the plea clear in her eyes.

Lynn glanced at Elliot, who wore a goofy grin. Gone was the embarrassment, and in swept the desire. She had no idea how to respond either. Being tongue-tied was no laughing matter. She wanted Elliot with them, but was it too soon?

"Mom, please? I want to open my presents while Elliot's there. I can't do that if he's not."

Apparently not. Not in Laura's eyes anyway. "Well, we can't have that. If Elliot wants to spend the night, then he's more than welcome to."

Elliot obviously needed no time to think about it. "I'd love to. I guess we'll see you tomorrow, Dad."

Gregory smiled, winking at Laura. "You better get an early shut-eye for Santa. I always made Elliot go to bed really early. He always woke us up really early, too."

"I can't wait for Santa! I will, Grandpa Gregory, I promise," Laura said as she ran over to him, hugging him tightly.

"That's my good girl. I have a few special presents for you under the tree at my house. I'll see you tomorrow," Gregory said, picking her up as he hugged her tightly back.

Elliot, Lynn, and Laura said goodbye to Gregory and Gabby, making it home ten minutes later. Laura kissed Lynn and Elliot on the cheek, said goodnight, and rushed off to bed to begin the wait for Santa.

Lynn clasped Elliot's hand, leading the way to her room. She shut her bedroom door and walked over to her dresser to grab her nightgown. "Do you need help undressing?" She turned toward Elliot, a small twinkle in her eye.

"Are you sure you want me sleeping in your room? Laura wanted me here, but maybe doesn't expect me in this room. I can sleep on the couch." He walked up to her, wrapping his arms around her.

"I think my daughter is smarter than we think. She

really likes you and Gregory. She called him grandpa. You have no idea what that means to me." She rested her head against his chest to hide the tears that wanted to escape.

"Shit, I'm sorry about my dad. I told him not to say things like that."

"That's not what I meant. She's never had anyone to call grandpa or grandma."

He kissed the top of her head as his warm, sweet touch soaked into her skin. Tiny tingles started to heat her up for what she knew was coming.

"My dad adores her. Just be warned, there are a lot of presents waiting for Laura at our house. My dad went a little crazy."

"She deserves it."

"So do you. I can't wait to give you your present." He grabbed her face and softly kissed her. "Let's go to bed. I have a feeling we'll be woken up really, really early."

She chuckled. "You have no idea."

They quickly got ready for bed and curled into a natural embrace within ten minutes. Not once did she look at the top of her closet. If she did, her mind would trail to a place she didn't want to go.

Elliot kissed her before saying goodnight. For the first time, he cradled her to his chest without going any further. She enjoyed this almost as much as she enjoyed the deep connection of intimacy.

She sensed the excitement in him about sharing Christmas morning with her and Laura. He came such a long way from that first day she met him in the diner. He didn't like the holiday then. Now, he seemed to almost enjoy it more than her.

They were almost a true family. And she wouldn't change a thing.

16

Elliot rubbed his eyes one more time before grinning at Laura, who squealed in delight at all the presents under the tree.

"Wow! Which one first? Which one first?" Laura started to pick up a present, lightly shook it, then moved to the next one.

"Just pick one and start, sweetheart." Lynn sat down next to Elliot on the couch, leaning into him as he wrapped his arms around her.

She moved her lips to his ear. "Where did those extra presents come from?"

He snatched a light kiss from her lips, then whispered back, "Santa."

She chuckled without a hint of irritation mingled in.

He hadn't known if she would get mad, but wanted to add to the joy of Santa coming. Thankfully, she didn't appear angry at him for adding three more presents under the tree. He had to sneak out in the middle of the night to add those presents to the pile. It hadn't been easy creeping out of bed without waking her up.

She reached for his hand, holding on to him like a lifeline. That's what he wanted. To be there for her. To cherish her. Cherish Laura. Sometimes, especially moments like this, it felt like everything was too good to be true. He'd never stop making her feel like a queen, like she was the only thing that mattered in the world. Because that's exactly how he felt. She was his everything.

He swore she was slipping away, especially when the worry still lingered in the depths of her eyes as she grabbed her robe hanging near her closet right before they joined Laura in the living room. He really had to find out what was bothering her.

"Oh my gosh! Oh my gosh! It's the monkey, Mom. The monkey!" Laura started hopping in her spot as she tore off the rest of the wrapping paper to reveal the talking monkey that Laura couldn't get enough of when they were in Wacky Wowza's.

"Keep opening more. You can play with everything when you're done. I want to see what else you got." Lynn laughed as Laura put on a brief pouty face that she couldn't just sit and play with the monkey, then grabbed another present to tear open.

Before long, Laura had opened every gift with eager excitement. She received the monkey, a monkey quilt, a CD from her favorite boy band, a makeup kit she had eyed in Wacky Wowza's, and the monkey watch Lynn had bought from the zoo. Those gifts came from Lynn.

Elliot gave her a small box that contained various card games, a sketchpad with colored pencils, and a gorgeous shirt that Laura had gushed over when they had been in Wacky Wowza's together. Each gift fit Laura to the T. He had taken the time to buy gifts that he knew Laura would enjoy. He had paid attention to everything Laura always said or did. He not only had to show Lynn how much he loved her, he had to let Laura know as well.

"Oh, wait. I have something for you guys." Laura jumped up from her spot, running to her room.

She came back with two presents wrapped somewhat messy. Globs of tape were slathered on one side where Laura probably got the tape stuck and decided just to leave it there. He couldn't help but smile at the cuteness of both gifts.

She handed one to Lynn, then the other to Elliot. "I hope you like them. I made them."

"You go first." Elliot nudged Lynn's shoulder. He needed a moment to regain his composure. He had the sudden need to shed a tear. A gift from Laura was unexpected. To think she had made him something hit him straight to the heart.

Lynn carefully unwrapped her present, taking her time. It must've started to annoy Laura because she grabbed part of the present and yanked on the paper. "You're supposed to do it fast, Mom. Not like a snail."

Lynn laughed as she helped tear the rest off. She tossed the paper to the floor, then carefully took the lid off the box. She pulled out the tissue paper and slowly revealed a beautiful butterfly made from clay. Laura had painted the center of the butterfly white, with the wings many different colors and tiny holes sprinkled around each wing.

"Do you like it? It's to hold your earrings. I made it in art class at school." Laura beamed with the brightest smile yet of the day.

"Like it? I love it. I love the colors. Thank you, sweetheart." Lynn hugged Laura tightly, then turned to Elliot. "Your turn."

His smile never wavered as he unwrapped his gift much faster than Lynn had. He dug through the tissue paper until he came across his clay figure. No words came. His smile morphed into a serious face as emotion clogged his throat.

"Do you like it, Elliot?" Laura asked softly.

Elliot cleared his throat as he stared at the figure of a baseball player holding a bat, poised in position to swing with vigor. He flipped it over to see the number 15 on the back of the jersey and smiled. Laura must've figured out that was his jersey number when he played as a teenager.

"It's the best present I've ever gotten. And you made it. That makes it even better." Elliot opened his arms for a hug as Laura wrapped her tiny body around his chest. "Thank you so much, Laura. You're the sweetest girl."

She sat back on the floor to play with her gifts, then looked over at Lynn. "I'm hungry, Mom."

"Breakfast coming right up." Lynn left the living room to make pancakes, while Elliot stayed on the couch.

He held the baseball figure in his hands, touched beyond words that Laura gave such a thoughtful gift. How had Laura known it would make him feel good? The baseball player was even painted in blue and red, the same colors his team wore when he was in high school. She thought of every last detail when she made it.

Every year his mother would buy him something baseball-like. It became such a tradition growing up that one year, when he was ten, he couldn't hide his disappointment when she didn't. His mom had never forgotten after that. It made him, for the first time since his mother passed away, feel a little closer to her.

"Elliot?" Laura said softly, standing next to him.

He glanced up from the figure. Her sweet smile melted his heart. "Yeah, my princess, what's the matter?"

"I just wanted to make sure you were okay. You look sad. You don't like my gift?"

"I love your gift. It reminds me of my mother, and that's one of the sweetest things you could've done. I miss her. Maybe that's why I look sad because it'd be nice if she were here."

"So I did good?" Laura asked brightly, wringing her hands nervously.

"You did wonderful. I can't wait to add this to my mantel in the living room. You can even help me pick out the perfect spot."

"Awesome!" Laura twirled around to resume her spot on the carpet by her toys when she turned back toward him. "I'm really glad Santa gave me the Christmas present I asked him for."

"Yeah, he's a smart guy. What present did he get right?" He wanted to tell Lynn to see her face light up with satisfaction.

"The perfect man for my mom. I asked Santa to find someone who would take care of my mom and make her happy. And right before Christmas, she met you."

Laura jumped into his arms, hugging him tightly. "You're part of our family now, Elliot, right? You won't ever leave. Because if you do, I think my mom would be very sad."

Elliot squeezed her back, words almost failing him—again. "I'll never leave. I love you and your mom too much to leave."

Laura let go, her eyes wide with happiness. "Really?"

"Yes, but you have to keep quiet," Elliot said, putting a finger to his lips. "I haven't told your mom yet. It's a surprise. I have something really special for her at my house."

"My lips are zipped." Laura twisted her fingers across her lips as if she was turning a key to lock something. "I love you, too, Elliot."

She went back to her toys on the carpet, barely registering when Elliot stood up slowly and walked out of the living room. His steps probably looked steady as he walked, but he felt far from steady. He had the approval and love from Laura. What a shock! And on Christmas morning that felt merry for the first time in a long time.

Now he just needed to have the love from Lynn as well.

His mouth curled with delight as Lynn swayed her hips to the Christmas music softly playing in the background as she prepared the pancakes. He loved watching her cook. He loved everything about her.

He planned to tell her later at his house. The perfect present waited patiently in his closet for her to open. His hands turned clammy as his heart started to pound. Those three little words played over and over on repeat. They fell out easily enough when he said it to Laura. Really easy, in fact. It shouldn't be too difficult with Lynn. For some reason, he was afraid the words would stall in his throat. He had to know what was bothering her. Yet, he didn't want to ruin such a beautiful morning.

He slowly approached her and wrapped her up as if he were afraid she would float away. "I could watch you all day in the kitchen. You make it impossible to resist you when you dance to the music like you do."

Lynn leaned back, sinking further into his embrace. "I like it when you can't resist me."

He kissed her neck, keeping it light, so he didn't suddenly pick her up and whisk her away to the bedroom. "I can't wait to take you to my house."

"Yeah. Why?"

"I have a present for you. I really want to give it to you now."

She turned around, cupping his cheeks. "I hope you didn't spend a lot. Stop spoiling me."

He kissed her lips. "I like spoiling you. It's never going to change. Let's eat, then head to my house."

"Are you really that impatient?" she asked with a laugh.

He grinned, grabbing another kiss. More like terrified. Would she like his present or kick him to the curb?

"I had no idea that Laura made you a gift. You really liked it, didn't you?"

"I love it." He kissed the top of her nose, then turned her back around to the stove, planting another soft kiss to her neck. "Chop, chop, we have a big day ahead of us."

She picked up her spatula, playfully swinging toward him. "Leave me be then, mister. No more distracting kisses."

He winked at her and walked out of the kitchen. Nothing but smiles on her face. Not even a trace of her worry. Odd. Why did he always see the worry when they were in her bedroom?

❄

"How is it you're cooking when it's our house?" Gregory asked Lynn as she dug through the cupboard looking for a certain spice.

"What can I say? I enjoy cooking. And I didn't really give you much of a choice. Gabby made lunch, which was delicious, by the way. Now I want to make supper." Lynn tilted her head as she smiled sweetly at him. "I really do enjoy cooking."

"I know better than to argue with a beautiful woman. I moved the car out of the garage. Gabby and I are going to take Laura to the garage so she can ride her bike. I don't want her to freeze outside or take a nasty spill because some snow is still covering the sidewalk."

Her face dipped slightly. "Her arm..."

"I'll keep her safe. Don't you worry about a thing."

Lynn chuckled. "It's a mother's job to worry. She really loves that new bike. Both you and Elliot spoiled her rotten. You guys really shouldn't have."

Gregory stepped closer to her, placing a warm hand on her shoulder. "I don't think that's going to change. Laura likes to call me grandpa. I hope that didn't make you mad."

"It made me want to cry, actually. She doesn't know her real grandparents. That's sad. I hope *you're* not mad."

He laughed heartily. "Nonsense. I love hearing it. I've been waiting forever for Elliot to settle down and give me some grandchildren. Lucky me, I don't have to wait nine months for one. I have one sitting in the living room right now. Doesn't get any better than that."

Lynn's eyes widened.

"Was that too forward? Elliot's always telling me to knock it off. You both just feel like family already."

"It's fine, Gregory. It's been one of the best Christmases I've ever had."

"And you've given me the best Christmas present ever. The light back in Elliot's eyes. I've missed my son." He kissed her cheek, then left her to finish preparing their supper.

He walked into the living room and saw Elliot pacing in the hallway. Laura and Gabby appeared oblivious to his obvious discomfort as they played a game on the floor. He made his way down the hallway.

"What's the matter, son?"

"What's Lynn doing?" Elliot ran a hand through his hair as he continued his small pacing.

"Cooking."

"I have one more present for her. I'm not sure I can give

it to her. What happens if she hates me for it and walks out?"

Gregory still looked confused. "I think you just need to stop worrying. How many times do I have to tell you that you worry too much?"

"I have to give her the present, Dad. I added a few things to it, though."

"What are you talking about?"

Elliot stopped pacing, glaring with frustration. "*The present*, Dad. The one that brought us together."

"Oh," Gregory said slowly. "Why do you even need to go there?"

"We talked about this. I'm not keeping it from her anymore."

"Right. Well, good luck. We're going biking in the garage." Gregory walked away before Elliot could say anything else.

❄

Elliot stood quietly in the hallway as his dad rounded up Laura and Gabby and vanished from his sight as they walked to the garage door. He took a deep breath before he made his way to the kitchen where Lynn stood on her tiptoes digging in the cupboard.

"Need help?"

Lynn glanced at him. "I've been digging in here for ages it seems like. Do you guys have chili powder?"

"Yeah, I'm pretty sure we do. I thought we were having chicken."

She smiled at him. "We are."

"Chili powder, hmm. What else is going on the chicken?"

"Wouldn't you like to know?" She turned back toward the cupboard as she laughed.

"Oh, some secret recipe, huh?"

"Yep, can't divulge my secret."

The pounding in his heart increased as he ran a hand through his hair. No more secrets. He couldn't take it anymore. Now was his chance. "I have one more present for you. It's been my secret for a while and I want to give it to you finally."

She turned around slowly, a frown appearing as she looked at him. "Elliot, you've given me so much. I don't need another present."

He walked over to her and grabbed her hand gently. "Last one, I promise. I just hope you like it and don't hate me for it."

She looked confused now, but laughed. It spilled from her lips, yet the laughter never reached her eyes. "Why would I hate you?"

"Come on." He pulled her hand to follow him to the bedroom.

When they walked in, he made her sit on the bed. He closed and locked the bedroom door, then went to his closet. He reached to the top shelf and removed the gift that had been hiding behind some shoeboxes.

Moment of truth. This was where his life turned into glorious bliss or pure hell. He blew out a breath and turned around. Could she see how badly his hands were shaking?

Lynn's eyes zoomed straight to the present. The same one she wrapped two weeks ago with wrapping paper she used to wrap all of her gifts with. The same one she had delicately tied with a red ribbon glistening with white snowflakes, just the way she tied all things. Like her apron.

"Elliot, is that my gift I gave to the church?" Her voice sounded unnatural.

"Yes."

She finally looked at him. "Did you know it was mine?"

"Yes."

He started to take a step toward her, stopping abruptly when the next words left her mouth.

"How in the hell did you get that? How long have you had it?"

Shit! He was losing her. Pure hell was making its way to his heart. He had no idea where to begin.

17

Elliot slowly walked to the bed as Lynn continued to stare at the gift with a blank expression. Deep silence filled the room. She had sounded mad when she demanded to know how he acquired the present, yet no anger had reached her beautiful face. Nothing had, really. Just complete emptiness. His heart plummeted to the floor, his hope right along with it.

He sat next to her and fiddled with the present. "I don't know where to start, but it's not what you think." He glanced at her. Still no emotion to give him any clues whether he'd survive this. "Not that I really know what you're thinking right now. You know why I'm really not a fan of Christmas. I came home one day for lunch and I saw this present sitting on the porch. It confused the hell out of me when I didn't see a name on it, but the words touched my heart."

Elliot withdrew the envelope from underneath the ribbon. There could be no mistaking the shakes in his hand now. Regardless of that, and the horrible silence from her, he read the card.

"May your holidays be ever bright. May your wishes be

ever right. May the spirit of Christmas fill you with love and comfort until the end of night."

He gazed at her with longing in his eyes. So much longing. He needed her to say something. Anything. Yet, she remained silent as she stared at the card in his hand. "I don't know what compelled me, but I opened the gift. When I found a pair of Christmas socks and some money inside, it confused me further. I asked my dad about it. He had no clue, but he said it must've been meant for me. I truly believe that now."

Finally, she lifted her eyes, a trace of passion lingering in the depths. Hope swelled for the first time. "My dad said it must've been donated to the church for a family in need. I insisted I didn't need anything. He said that maybe I was in need of a lot of things and told me to figure out who donated the gift if I was so hell-bent on returning it. I searched every church in the surrounding area until I came across Mason and Father Preston."

"He told you it was from me?" Lynn whispered as her hands clenched tightly.

Elliot gave a strangled laugh. "He recognized your gift, but refused to tell me who it was from. I didn't care at the time. I tried to make him take it back and he simply wouldn't listen to me. Then he asked if I would drop off the donation box at the diner. That's where I met you."

He gripped the present in one hand. Her eyes started to sparkle. At last, her emotion was shining through. Just not the kind he wanted to see. More sadness than passion. How in the hell did he reverse that?

Instinctively, he grabbed one of her hands and clung tightly. She had to understand. He needed her to love him as much as he loved her.

"You took my breath away, Lynn. You had me speechless

from the onset. That's never happened to me before. I didn't want to order a damn thing. I just wanted you to sit down and talk with me. I didn't connect the present until I saw the ribbon in your hair and the note you left on the check. I knew then the gift had to come from you."

"Why didn't you give it to me then? Why...." She glanced away, but thankfully didn't physically pull away. Although, she had yet to grip his hand back. Things were still not looking bright and merry.

"Lynn, don't hold back. Please. Say anything." *Like, I forgive you. I love you.* Only in his dreams, apparently.

"Why play games with me?"

He squeezed her hand, then lightly pressed a tender kiss to it. "I have never played games with you."

She sucked in a breath as tears glistened in the corner of her eyes. "But you wanted to know what kind of gift to donate to the church. Why ask me something like that?"

"I panicked. I thought about telling you I had your gift and giving it back, but I didn't think you'd like that. You're a proud woman. You work so hard to provide for Laura. You work too damn much if you ask me. And no matter how much you work, you're still low on cash. Yet, you donated."

He lifted the gift as his smile grew. "Remember what you said to me when I asked what you donated?"

She shook her head. "Not really."

He caressed the top of her hand with his thumb. A slight tremble erupted from her. A sign of hope. At least, that's how his aching heart interpreted it.

"Give something that shows the Christmas spirit, that can last a lifetime if properly cared for, and can keep you warm at night." He laughed lightly. "You were describing a pair of socks, quite beautifully."

He kissed the top of her hand. She made no move to pull

away. His hope continued to rise, especially when the tiny tremors still escaped when he touched her in any little way.

"Please don't be mad. I've been so afraid that I'd lose you over it. I don't care how this gift landed on my porch, but it's the best damn gift I've ever received. It brought me to you. You gave me exactly what I wanted."

He inhaled a sharp breath. "You give me the Christmas spirit, which makes me want to give you the best Christmas experience back. If you let me, I will love you for a lifetime. Forever. And care for you until the day I die. I will always keep you warm at night. Having you in my arms feels perfect and right. That's my last gift to you. Exactly what you said I should find to give. And I found it. Right in front of me. I love you, Lynn. I love your beautiful daughter."

A tear slid down her cheek.

"Don't cry. Do anything but that." He set the gift on her lap and wiped the tear away. "Open it."

Her bottom lip trembled as she eyed the gift. "It's your gift. I don't want it back. You were right. I would've been offended."

He cupped her face, rubbing a tender thumb across her cheek as he wiped another tear away. "It's our gift now. I added something."

He dropped his hands to his lap and waited for her to open the gift. She hadn't said anything about his declaration of love. That didn't mean she didn't love him. But it had been like a punch to the gut. He couldn't lose her now. Not when he knew what love truly felt like.

❄

LYNN WIPED ANOTHER TEAR AWAY. Crying wouldn't solve this, or mend the wounds. His soft touch had done a better job of that. Perhaps they were more like tears of joy. Her emotions were so entwined with confusion—and guilt. He poured his heart out. Every time she chanced a glance at him, she couldn't help but cry. His love flowed out in waves. She should tell him what was in her heart.

She picked up the gift and carefully untied the bow, then started to rip the wrapping paper open with the same careful precision she always did when opening a gift. Laura would most likely chastise her for going so slow. Rushing seemed impossible. The fear tingled in her fingertips. What could've he possibly added to the gift?

Temptation almost overwhelmed her to fold the wrapping paper, but she set it aside instead. Delaying the inevitable wouldn't make it go away. She needed to find out what he added. Then she needed to confess everything.

Her lips curled softly as she pulled off the lid to see the socks lying on top. Her cheeks flamed with heat. She should've thought of a better gift than this. What had he really thought when he first opened it? Perhaps how pathetic of a gift it was.

She risked a furtive glance at him. The love still sparkled brightly, along with a small amount of worry.

She pulled the socks out, crinkling her eyebrows at the red and white hat that lay underneath. She lifted the hat, immediately slapping a hand to her mouth. A giggle escaped.

Pink fluffy handcuffs.

"I thought it all would look lovely on you," Elliot whispered.

Her eyes darted to his concerned, handsome face. His hand slid off his leg to the bed. Yet, he didn't touch her.

"Pink does look nice on me," she said with a small

chuckle. "I don't really have anything that matches the socks or the hat."

He leaned toward her ear, his warm breath tickling her senses. "I don't want you wearing anything but the socks and hat. That's the point." He kissed her neck before going back to his original position.

Red-hot shivers rushed down her spine as his love sparked within her. "We'll have to return the handcuffs."

He reached for the cuffs and twirled them. "You wanted these. I've been imagining quite a few things to do with them."

"I already bought a pair for us."

His eyes flashed brightly with desire. "A woman after my own heart. Is that what's hidden in your closet?"

Guilt swooped back in. She averted her eyes as she clutched the hat and socks.

"You have my heart, Lynn. Why do I get the feeling I don't have yours?"

"Do you want to know how I got the money to pay you for my car?"

His warm hand slid down her arm and grabbed her hand. "It doesn't matter. Hell, I think I'd look the other way if you did rob a bank."

Her head whipped toward him as a laugh escaped. "You don't mean that."

"Don't I?" His eyes shimmered with so much love, sprinkled with a bit of laughter.

"I loved Trent. He was my everything. I felt so lost when he died." Geez, why did she blurt it out like that? Although, her heart felt ten times lighter already.

The amusement in his eyes died, as did the love, replaced with a terrifying panic. "So, you can't possibly love me like you did with him?" He reached for the box. "Maybe you should give that back."

She dropped the socks and hat and swiped the box before he could grab it. Her hand tightened on his, gripping so hard she saw his confusion. "I sold the engagement ring he gave me."

"You're killing me here."

"I decided it was time to make some space in my closet... or more like, in my heart. You mean everything to me, Elliot. I let him go to let you in. I just didn't know how to tell you that."

He cocked his lip in his usual charming smile, the light filling back up in his eyes. "There's one more thing left in the box."

"Do you understand now?"

He squeezed her hand back. "You didn't completely let his love go, but you made more room for me. I understand that. I really think you should finish opening your gift."

"Right. The twenty dollar bill."

"No. I spent the twenty." He twirled the handcuffs as he grinned at her. "I have a few more things tucked away in my closet. Just like you do at your house."

She lightly laughed. Maybe she hadn't donated such a pathetic gift, at least, not when Elliot was the recipient.

Fate.

She didn't know what possessed her in the first place to toss the socks in the box.

Her heart felt free and light as she pulled out the tissue paper lining the bottom of the box. Elliot had it right. She hadn't stopped loving Trent. She just moved him to the side to let Elliot's love in. It all felt completely right.

But what did he want her to see? There was nothing else inside the box. She started to put the tissue paper back inside when something small fell to her lap. Her jaw dropped.

Her fingers shook with awe as she picked up the diamond ring.

Elliot dropped to the floor, bending on one knee. He grabbed her hand that held the diamond ring. "I love you, Lynn. I would never ask you to forget about him or throw his love away. Now I know why you were so worried these last few days. From here on out, no more secrets from either of us. I didn't mean to keep it a secret for so long. I wanted everything to be perfect. Give me one more gift. The gift of your heart, like I've given mine. Marry me?"

No hesitation whatsoever. She immediately launched herself into his arms. He inhaled sharply. "Oh, I forgot, Elliot. I'm sorry about your shoulder."

He held her tightly when she tried to leave his arms. "You didn't answer me. Will you marry me?"

She buried her head into his neck as she whispered, "I love you, Elliot. I can't imagine being anywhere else but in your arms. Yes, I'll marry you."

His hot breath touched her very soul. "I love you so damn much."

She lifted her head, clutched his face, and kissed him senseless. Her legs wrapped around his waist, seeking his heat as she tangled her tongue with his. The love swirled between them. Devouring him sounded like a very good idea. He seemed to agree as the kiss became stronger, his hands combing through her hair and down her back in a tantalizing caress.

Abruptly, she pulled away, breathing deeply. Ripping all of his clothes off and having him deep inside her on the bedroom floor couldn't happen right now. The house wasn't empty. "We should go tell the others the good news."

He claimed her lips again, stroking his fingers up and down her back, then clutched the hem of her sweater. "We can tell them later. My dad knows that I was giving you one more present. The bedroom door is locked. Let me love you, Lynn. Put your Christmas present on for me."

She giggled as she turned her head to the socks and hat lying on the bed. "You want me to put that on. What happens if they hear us?"

He kissed her neck, trailing a line of kisses to her ear. She couldn't help but open her neck for more. "They're in the garage. They won't hear a thing. I want to show my fiancé just what she means to me."

She smiled as the heat intensified between them. "Fiancé. I like the sound of that."

He drew her sweater up and over her head and tossed it behind him. Her bra disappeared next with quiet ease. He reached behind her and grabbed the hat, placing it on top of her head. Stroking the strands of her hair, he started to frame it all in a beautiful manner.

She couldn't take it anymore. His touch made her ache for immediate release. She wanted this to last for as long as possible.

"I'll finish the rest. Get naked, mister," she said as she stood up.

❄

ELLIOT WHIPPED OFF HIS CLOTHES, his eyes never once leaving her gorgeous movements as she undid her pants and slid the socks on. Provocatively, one at a time. She jumped onto the bed, positioning herself in the middle by propping her hand to her cheek, resting her elbow deep into the mattress. She crossed her feet, then slowly stroked one foot over her other leg all the way to her knee as she gave him a come-hither smile.

Damn luckiest guy in the world. How had he gotten so lucky?

A simple present left on his porch.

"Merry Christmas, Elliot. Come get your last gift," she said with a glowing smile.

He'd never hate Christmas again. Not when he received gifts like this.

Lynn continued with the sultry looks, stroking her hand down her side. Enticing him. Making him yearn for her. Everything was exactly how he pictured. Lynn gloriously naked, and oh so beautiful. She was everything that he could've asked for. He joined her on the bed and pulled her into his loving arms.

Best Christmas present ever.

❄

Don't miss the rest of this heartwarming holiday series!

Mistletoe Magic
Christmas Wish
Snowed in Love
Snowflakes and Shots

For Aiden & Theresa's story
Mistletoe Magic
A Holiday Romance Novel - Book 2

A mistletoe. A kiss. This just might be the start of a beautiful Christmas.

Theresa might not make the best pot of coffee in town, but people still flock to the diner for a cup, even Officer Crowl, who rarely displays a smile since his fiancé died. She'll never be able to win his heart, but it's hard to resist him, especially when he kisses her under the mistletoe. Well, on the cheek, but that has to count for something…right?

Staying busy keeps Officer Aiden Crowl sane. Because when he's idle or alone, he thinks, and nothing good comes from that. Everyone thinks he was the perfect man. They think he's broken because she's gone. He is, just not for the reason they believe. Every time he walks into the diner, one sweet smile from Theresa erases some of the pain. He should stay away from her. Far away. But what is he supposed to do when they're standing under a mistletoe? Kiss her, of course.

For Bentley & Emma's story
Christmas Wish
A Holiday Romance Novel - Book 3

What if you had one wish granted for Christmas? What would it be?

Acting reckless isn't something Bentley Wilson is known for, but when he runs back into a burning building to save a little girl's puppy after specifically told not to do so, that's exactly how most of the town sees him, especially the fire chief who insists he has to help with the annual Christmas party because of his behavior. Throw in the fact the woman he pined over for too long is getting married, this holiday is going to go down as one of the worst. Until he meets Emma Brookes. She's feisty, headstrong, and holds so much pain hidden in the depths of her beautiful green eyes. He wants nothing more than to erase her sadness. But it's already a season of disaster, and every time they're together, they spar like two warriors dueling to the death. Despite that, he likes the challenge, the crazy way she makes him feel. Before the holiday is up, he vows to get his one Christmas wish. That she never leaves his side.

For James & Erin's story
SNOWED IN LOVE
A HOLIDAY ROMANCE NOVEL - BOOK 4

A blizzard. A cabin. A cup of hot chocolate.
The perfect mixture to fall in love.

James Brennen is nothing but a screwup. At least, in the small town of Mulberry, that's what everyone thinks of him. As a recovering alcoholic, he's trying his best to turn his life around, to be a better man. All of his hard work comes crashing down when he's fired from his job at the hospital— accused of stealing drugs. Nothing ever changes and he's done trying to prove himself. Needing time alone, his friend's cabin in the middle of the woods provides the perfect escape. He knows he's found deep trouble, not only when he gets stranded during a brutal snowstorm, but that he's stuck with the one woman he's wanted since the first day he laid eyes on her. The passion burns bright between them, but it doesn't matter, as soon as Christmas is over, he's leaving for good.

FOR STU & CHASITY'S STORY
SNOWFLAKES AND SHOTS
A HOLIDAY ROMANCE NOVEL - BOOK 5

One last shot at love...

Stu doesn't have many regrets in life—not even the fact he never decorates his bar for the holidays. But when a bar fight turns into needing medical attention, he's put face-to-face with the one woman he's tried to avoid for the last fifteen years. Okay, so maybe he regrets a few things. He should've never walked away from her. It only took a good knock to his head to make him see clearly. He's going to win Chasity's heart once again. It doesn't matter that she's not going to make it easy; he's up for the challenge. Bring on the bets and all the Christmas spirit he can handle. Except, one person doesn't like the idea of them together—the same person that had him walking away from her all those years ago.

ABOUT THE AUTHOR

I'm a *USA Today* Bestselling Author that loves to write sweet contemporary romance and romantic suspense novels, although I am partial to romantic suspense. Honestly, I love anything that has to do with romance. As long as there's a happy ending, I'm a happy camper. And insta-love...yes, please! I love baseball (Go Twins!) and creating awesome crafts. I graduated with a Bachelor's Degree in Criminal Justice, working in that field for several years before I became a stay-at-home mom. I have a few more amazing stories in the works. If you would like to connect with me or see important news, head to my website at http://www.amandasiegrist.com. Thanks for reading!

Made in the USA
Columbia, SC
03 November 2020